Butterfly;
Signature of a Serial Killer

R. Leonowicz

COPYRIGHT © 2025

All rights are reserved. No part of this book may be reproduced, distributed, or transmitted in any form or by any means, including photocopying, recording, or other electronic or mechanical methods, without the prior written permission of the author, except in the case of brief quotations embodied in critical reviews and certain other noncommercial uses permitted by copyright law. For permission requests, write to the author at the address provided in the acknowledgments section of this book.

Printed in the United States of America

First Printing Edition, 2025

ISBN: 9798294617110

Dedication

Special thanks to my colleagues at Methodist Children s Hospital, especially those I had the privilege of working alongside on the Pediatric and Neonatal Specialized Air Medical Team.

I am also deeply grateful to the countless healthcare professionals and police officers who show up every day, risking so much in service to others. The silent burdens they carry, the pain, the trauma, the memories, which often remain unseen as they protect others from the harsh realities they endure. Your strength and sacrifice do not go unnoticed.

Author's Note

Butterfly: A Signature of a Serial Killer was first brought to life over 20 years ago, during my time as a young registered respiratory therapist working full-time. Though the novel is fictional, many of the events and emotions woven into the story are drawn from real experiences I witnessed throughout my career, adapted and altered to stay true to the characters and their journey.

Nicole, one of the two central characters, hides her identity as a lesbian from her coworkers, reflecting the social climate of the time when the original manuscript was written. After retiring, I decided to revisit and breathe new life into the story, giving it a fresh beginning.

The upcoming sequel will explore Nicole's journey as she navigates life openly gay, facing the challenges of love, friendship, and identity. At its heart, it remains a gripping mystery, one that will keep you turning page after page.

Table of Contents

Chapter One 1

Chapter Two 14

Chapter Three 31

Chapter Four 38

Chapter Five 50

Chapter Six 61

Chapter Seven 69

Chapter Eight 75

Chapter Nine 84

Chapter Ten 93

Chapter Eleven 98

Chapter Twelve 103

Chapter Thirteen 110

Chapter Fourteen 128

Chapter Fifteen 136

Chapter Sixteen 140

Chapter Seventeen.. 146

Chapter Eighteen.. 154

Chapter Nineteen.. 162

Chapter Twenty 171

Chapter Twenty One 187

Chapter Twenty Two 197

CHAPTER ONE

The full moon glistened on the wet pavement of a dimly lit backstreet in downtown San Antonio. A fine mist lingered in the cool night breeze, adding to the eerie stillness. Dirty windows and damp concrete reflected the flashing red and blue lights of police cruisers, casting an ominous glow over the narrow alley. Several squad cars blocked both ends of the passage as uniformed officers rushed to secure the scene. Thick yellow tape cordoned off a section near a large commercial dumpster, where a man s lifeless body lay sprawled in a pool of blood. Against the brick wall, a woman in her late forties sat crouched, sobbing. Her tawny hair, damp and disheveled, clung to her tear-streaked face. Blood trickled from a gash on her forehead, smearing with the black mascara and crimson lipstick streaked across her cheek. She wore a long black satin dress, now wet and mud-streaked from the dirty pavement. One sleeve had been torn away, exposing a black lace bra and silk slip. A large gash ran from her elbow to her wrist, the blood seeping onto her trembling fingers. A police officer knelt beside her, pressing a towel against the cut to control the bleeding.

The wail of ambulance sirens faded as the vehicle pulled into the narrow alley, coming to a sharp stop. The front doors swung open, and two paramedics, Maggie Reed and Nicole McBride, stepped out, quickly grabbing their equipment from the back of the unit. They moved toward the woman slumped against the wall, but before they could reach her, Lieutenant Bob Mitchell of the Homicide Division intercepted them.

Maggie recognized him immediately.

What do we have here, Bob?" she asked.

Male, late forties—stab wounds to the neck and chest. Officers found him unresponsive and pulseless when they arrived. Nothing we could do," Mitchell said, coughing into his hand. His wife is over there. She's cut up pretty bad."

Maggie glanced at the woman. What's her name?"

Patricia Castle," Mitchell replied. She was on her way to meet her husband. He was working late in the Keller Building across the street. They were supposed to have dinner together. As she approached the building, some guy grabbed her from behind, put a knife to her throat, and dragged her into the alley. He tried to rape her, but her husband saw what was happening. Instead of calling for help, he ran after them—and now here we are."

The paramedics exchanged a quick look before kneeling beside Patricia and setting their equipment down.

Mrs. Castle, I'm Maggie from Emergency Medical Services, and this is Nicole. We're here to help you," Maggie said gently as she reached to check the wound on Patricia's arm. The moment she lifted the towel, fresh blood seeped from the torn flesh.

Patricia jerked away. No... please, I'm fine," she sobbed. Please, do something for my husband! He's over there!" Her voice broke as she pointed frantically toward the dumpster. Please... I beg you! No one will help him!"

Maggie caught Patricia's arm, holding her back.

Yes, of course," Maggie said gently. Nicole and Lieutenant Mitchell will check on your husband. But you need to let me help you, alright?"

Patricia hesitated, then, exhausted, she gave a small nod. "Alright... Thank you. Thank you for helping." Tears streamed down her face as she spoke.

Maggie quickly assessed Patricia's injuries, carefully bandaging the deep wound on her arm before tending to the gash on her forehead. She checked her vital signs, speaking to her in a calm, reassuring tone as she worked.

As Maggie continued treating her, a detective arrived on the scene. He introduced himself as Detective Rick Mallory. Though Maggie recognized him from previous crime scenes, they were only vaguely acquainted. He crouched beside Patricia and began asking for details about the attack.

A few minutes later, Nicole returned with a stretcher.

"How is he? Will he be alright?" Patricia's voice wavered with fragile hope.

Nicole hesitated before answering. "I'm so sorry... his injuries were too severe. He died instantly from the knife wound. There was nothing we could do."

"No... no," Patricia whispered, her voice breaking as she buried her face in her hands and sobbed.

Maggie exchanged a look with the detective. "We're ready to go now. She needs further care. You can finish your questions on the way."

Without waiting for a response, she gently helped Patricia onto the stretcher, secured the straps, and gathered her equipment.

As the ambulance pulled away, Maggie rode in the back with the grieving woman, closely monitoring her vitals. Detective Mallory sat across from them, quietly continuing his questioning. Patricia, her body trembling, recounted the horrific events between gasping sobs. Maggie listened, offering quiet reassurances as they made their way to University Hospital.

Mrs. Castle, it s essential that we get a description of the man who did this to you and your husband," Detective Mallory said in a somber tone. Did you see his face? What sort of clothing was he wearing?"

Patricia sat strapped to the stretcher, her arms drawn tightly to her chest. Shock had consumed her, and she stared vacantly out the back window, watching the city lights blur as the ambulance sped through the streets of San Antonio.

After a long silence, she finally spoke. Yes... I saw his face." Her voice was distant, trembling. He was white, maybe in his late twenties. He had blonde hair. I... I didn t see the color of his eyes. I think they were dark. He looked so... normal." She choked back a sob, then suddenly broke down. Oh my God, how could this happen?"

Maggie reached out, gently placing a hand on Patricia s arm. She offered her a cloth to wipe her tears. Take your time," she said softly.

The detective pressed on, his voice steady but urgent. What about his height or weight? Any distinguishing marks—tattoos, scars?"

Patricia shook her head, struggling to gather her thoughts. No... I don t know. It happened so fast." She swallowed hard, her voice barely above a whisper. I guess he was about Peter s height... six foot? Maybe 200 pounds? But I—I m not sure."

She suddenly gasped, her breath hitching. The kids... I need to call my—" But the words never came. Instead, her body trembled, and she dissolved into sobs once more.

Detective Mallory leaned forward, elbows resting on his knees, his eyes fixed on his notepad. He started to click the end of his pen open and shut; an annoying habit that surfaced when he was stuck in the plight of trying to get a statement from a victim. He straightened his back against the seat, his expression jaded and distant. Maggie glanced at him, studying the wear etched into his face. The deep-set wrinkles on his forehead, the frown lines around his mouth, and the streaks of gray in his brown hair painted a picture of a man weighed down by years of violence and tragedy. He tried to mask it—tried to maintain an air of compassion—but Maggie could see past it. His heart had grown distant, numbed by the endless cycle of crime and suffering.

She understood it all too well. Even in her profession, the constant exposure to pain and loss could corrode a person's spirit. It was a slow unraveling, one that seeped into every corner of life if left unchecked.

"We're almost there, Mrs. Castle," she said gently. "I need to ask you a few more questions." Maggie hesitated, bracing herself for the next one. It was a painful thing to ask, but it was necessary for both medical and legal reasons. Her voice softened further.

"Did the man rape you?"

The question hung in the air, heavy and unbearable.

"No... he tried," Patricia whispered, her voice trembling. "He pulled me behind the dumpster, held a knife to my throat, and pinned me against the wall. He started tearing at my dress." Her breath hitched, and she squeezed her eyes shut as if trying to block out the memory.

"Then Peter came around the corner. He was calling my name." Her lips quivered as she continued. "The man covered my mouth with his hand. It oozed an odor of garbage." She shook her head in disbelief, as though recounting someone else's nightmare.

Her fingers clutched the edge of the stretcher. "He threw me to the ground while he and Peter fought. But then, he stabbed him, just like that. Peter—he fell. He never got back up." Her voice cracked. "I should have helped. I should have run. But I was so scared... all I could do was watch." She shuddered. "It was horrible."

Maggie placed a reassuring hand on her shoulder, but Patricia hardly noticed. Her mind was trapped in the horror of that night.

"He came back toward me and started tearing at my clothes again. He was saying something... I—I could barely hear him." She hesitated, her brow furrowed. "He said something like butterfly.'" Her glassy eyes lifted to meet Maggie's. "Isn't that strange? Butterfly. Why would he say that?"

Tears spilled down her cheeks, black rivulets of mascara tracing the path of her anguish. Her voice grew weaker, barely a whisper. "I heard voices from the alleyway. I think someone must have heard the fight because he ran off. That's all I remember." She swallowed hard. "He called me his little butterfly, I could feel the brush of his breath on my neck."

And then, she broke down again, sobbing uncontrollably.

Maggie stole a glance at Detective Mallory. He kept writing, but for a split second, his hand hesitated. His jaw tightened. That one word—butterfly—confirmed what he had feared.

The same MO.

For the past three months, five rapes had been reported, all with an unsettling detail: every victim said their attacker had called them butterfly. The cases remained unsolved. But this time, the attack had been interrupted, which could have provoked the assailant to murder.

All the previous rape victims had given the same description of the assailant: a white male, appearing to be in his late twenties. Each had explicitly recalled his voice, the chilling word butterfly which appeared to be his signature.

His pattern was disturbingly consistent. He struck within the inner city, always between seven and ten o'clock at night. Maggie and Nicole had been on duty during the nights of the other reported rapes, making them all too familiar with the case.

The police had not released any statement to the media in connection with the rapes. The police chief feared that public panic would jeopardize the investigation. Instead, the city police department had vaguely reported an increase in sexual assaults, advising women to be more cautious and avoid traveling alone at night.

The ambulance pulled into the emergency bay, its tires steady against the wet pavement as it stopped in front of the ER. Maggie and Nicole moved swiftly, guiding the stretcher through the automatic doors leading into the triage area.

A young man in blue hospital scrubs met them at the entrance.

Treatment room one," he said, pointing toward a side room.

Thanks, Bill," Maggie replied, steering the stretcher in the designated direction.

As Nicole continued pushing the stretcher, Maggie paused in the hallway to give a quick report.

Patient s name is Patricia Castle, 48-year-old female, assault victim—attempted rape. She s extremely anxious, alert and oriented. Vitals: heart rate 130, respirations 26, blood pressure 164 over 100 and oxygen saturation is 98%. She has a deep laceration on her right lateral forearm, extending from her elbow to her wrist, plus an abrasion on her forehead and several bruises. No other deformities noted." I.V. started enroute 5mg Morphine given for pain and anxiety." She took a breath before adding, The assault was interrupted before the rape occurred. Her husband witnessed the attack and intervened. He sustained fatal stab wounds at the scene."

Maggie s voice softened. It s... not a good situation. The detectives are probably on their way here to collect any DNA samples she might have on her. Remember to bag her clothes properly."

"All right, Maggie, I think that's all I need," Bill said, closing his clipboard. Then, with a smirk, he added, "How are things going with you?"

Maggie exhaled, rubbing her temples. "Alright, I suppose. Just tired—it's been a long night." She ran a hand through her thick, wavy hair, pushing it out of her face.

Bill chuckled. "What about your pretty partner? Still single? You know, you should really put in a good word for me."

Maggie rolled her eyes but smirked. "Gotcha, Bill. I'll see you later."

She gave him a quick wave and turned to find Nicole, who was already heading toward the nurse's station.

"I'm gonna grab a cup of coffee," Nicole called over her shoulder. "You want one?"

Maggie shook her head. "No thanks. I actually want to sleep tonight—no more caffeine for me."

With that, she pushed through the automatic doors and made her way back to the ambulance. Climbing into the passenger seat, she let out a deep breath and grabbed her clipboard. With their shift ending in an hour, she wanted to finish the paperwork so she could leave on time. The rhythmic scratching of her pen filled the quiet cabin as she documented Patricia Castle's injuries and the events of the night.

A few minutes later, Nicole returned, coffee in hand. She climbed into the back of the ambulance and started cleaning up the equipment. Neither of them spoke; they didn't need to. After two years of working side by side, they had developed an unspoken rhythm—a partnership built on trust, instinct, and a shared understanding of the weight their job carried.

Nicole, only twenty-eight—just a year younger than Maggie—had started as a volunteer for the city fire department while attending school. After earning her paramedic certification, she applied to the San Antonio City ambulance service, where Maggie became her mentor.

Maggie finished the last of the paperwork and glanced through the small dividing window into the back of the ambulance. Nicole was still cleaning, moving with the efficiency of someone who had done this routine a hundred times. Maggie hesitated, watching her for a moment, her thoughts drifting back to what Bill had said. Pretty and single. If only he knew.

She studied Nicole—the sharp contrast of her jet-black hair against her pale skin, the delicate arch of her finely trimmed eyebrows that framed her deep gray-blue eyes. The dimples on either side of her mouth were visible even when she wasn't smiling. With her athletic frame and toned arms, she looked strong, capable. Maggie remembered the day Nicole had confided in her about being a lesbian. Other than Maggie and Nicole's brother, Gary, no one else knew. It wasn't something Nicole flaunted, nor did she hide it—she simply lived her life.

Maggie smiled softly and leaned her head against the seat, still watching as Nicole wiped down the stretcher. After a moment, Nicole caught her staring.

"You know you want me," Nicole teased, tossing a towel in Maggie's direction.

Maggie rolled her eyes and swatted it away. "Only in your dreams."

Nicole smirked but quickly picked up on Maggie's distant expression. Her tone shifted. "Alright, what's on your mind? You look lost in thought."

"Nothing," Maggie said, stretching her arms with a sigh. "Just counting the minutes until our shift is over." She hesitated, then smirked.

By the way, Bill asked about you again tonight. You should go out with him. Give up on silly women—we re all crazy and hormonal anyway."

Nicole didn t respond right away. Instead, she climbed out of the back of the ambulance, shut the doors, and walked around to the driver s side. Sliding into her seat, she started the engine.

Maggie turned toward her, still smiling. What? I m just curious. You re a sweet girl, way too cute to be alone."

Nicole exhaled, shaking her head. We ve been through this before. I m not looking for anyone right now—especially a guy." She paused, then glanced sideways at Maggie, lifting an eyebrow.

It was her unspoken signal—time to drop the subject.

Maggie held up her hands in surrender. Alright, alright." She sighed, resting her head back against the seat.

What do you think? Let s call it a day and head back to the station." Nicole turned the key in the ignition, shifted the gear, and pulled out of the ambulance bay. The city lights blurred past them, but Maggie s thoughts lingered. She sat in silence, her gaze fixed out the side window. The darkness outside stretched endlessly, mirroring the weight in her chest.

Some nights, the weight of their job felt heavier than others. And some things, no matter how much they joked or deflected, always remained just beneath the surface. Her thoughts drifted back to Patricia Castle—the shattered woman they had just left in the emergency room. In mere minutes, her life had been torn apart. She had lost her husband, the man who had tried to protect her.

Maggie swallowed hard. She couldn t help but wonder... what if it had been Victor?

She met him at a cooking workshop—an unexpected place for romance, but fate worked in strange ways. Victor had been a widower, still struggling to move forward after losing his first wife in a tragic scuba diving accident. Two years had passed, and he hadn't quite adjusted to life without her, so he started attending workshops to meet new people.

At first, Maggie hadn't thought of him as conventionally attractive—tall, with dishwater blonde hair and warm brown eyes. But there was something about his presence. His quiet strength. His kindness. She had been drawn to him in ways she didn't expect.

Their love had come fast, unexpected, but real. Now, only a few years into their marriage, the demands of her third-shift job had already started to wear on their relationship. The late nights. The exhaustion. The missed moments. Yet, even through the struggles, she couldn't imagine life without him. And tonight, after seeing Patricia's anguish, she felt an overwhelming sorrow.

"What's troubling you?" Nicole's voice pulled her from her thoughts.

Maggie exhaled, shaking her head. "Just thinking about the last case we dropped off. Her attacker... it looks like he's the same man who assaulted the other women in the area."

Nicole's grip tightened on the steering wheel. "How do you know?"

"Each woman told Mallory the attacker called them his butterfly."

Nicole frowned. "That's insane. I hope they catch the guy soon."

The ambulance turned into the station's lot, rolling into its usual spot alongside several other emergency vehicles. Nicole cut the engine and lingered, her hand resting on the door handle.

"Wanna grab a beer? Shoot some pool? Just chill for a bit before heading home?"

Maggie turned toward her, offering a tired smile. She already knew Nicole expected her to say no, but still, she asked. And Maggie appreciated that.

Maggie reached over and patted Nicole's shoulder before sliding her tired body out of the ambulance. She stifled a yawn as she made her way to the locker room, dropping her gear inside before grabbing her purse and car keys. With a final glance at the time clock, she punched out.

Nicole, meanwhile, turned in the ambulance keys and gave a quick report to the shift operator before heading home.

The night air was cool against Maggie's skin as she stepped outside. She drove the short distance to her townhome, her black BMW gliding smoothly into the garage beside Victor's red Ford pickup. The sight of his truck should have brought her comfort, but instead, it reminded her of how little time they spent together.

Inside, the house was dark except for the faint glow of the hallway nightlight. She moved quietly, careful not to disturb the silence. The townhouse had been a dream purchase—a three-bedroom, two-bath home in the medical center district, centrally located for both of their jobs. It had made sense at the time. A practical choice. But with Victor working a nine-to-five job as a financial advisor and Maggie on the three-to-eleven shift, their paths barely crossed these days.

Maggie hurried into the bathroom, shutting the door before turning on the light. The bright glow made her squint. She turned on the bathtub faucet, letting the water run as she leaned against the sink and stared at her reflection.

Fatigue weighed on her features. She traced a hand down her cheek, her smooth skin a small victory after years of childhood acne. Her sky-blue eyes stood out against her lightly sun-kissed skin, a result of her afternoon walks. Thick, dark brown hair framed her face, a little longer than she liked. Her bangs were starting to fall into her eyes. She exhaled, stretching her arms before reaching over to turn off the water. Stripping off her clothes, she slid into the bath, letting the warmth soak into her sore muscles. The heat wrapped around her like a cocoon, easing away the tension of the day.

After her bath, she slipped into her two-piece silk pajamas and shuffled into the bedroom. The room was cloaked in darkness, except for the faint glow from the nightlight in the hall. Victor lay beneath the covers, his form still and steady. Maggie hesitated for a moment before climbing into bed. The mattress dipped slightly as she settled in, her body sinking into the familiar softness. She reached out, resting a gentle hand on Victor's back.

Victor, are you awake?" she whispered.

Silence.

She waited, feeling the steady rise and fall of his breathing beneath her fingertips. He didn't move. He didn't answer.

Maggie sighed softly but didn't pull her hand away. If he was asleep, she didn't want to wake him. Yet something kept her there, watching, waiting.

Her eyes fluttered closed, exhaustion pulling her under.

In the darkness, Victor opened his eyes. He remained silent, staring into the void, before slowly closing them again.

CHAPTER TWO

Bright sunlight filtered through the floral curtains, casting soft patterns across the room. Maggie lay buried beneath the sheets and comforter, reluctant to leave the warmth of her cocoon. The morning had already slipped away, yet even after more than eight hours of sleep, her body still felt drained.

She pushed the comforter down, allowing the cool air to brush against her skin, reviving her senses. Turning her head, she stared at the empty side of the bed. Victor was already gone. A frown flickered across her face as she reached out, fingers grazing his pillow. He hadn't woken her to say goodbye as he usually did.

As she shifted to sit up, she felt the bed tremble slightly as she glanced down toward her feet—two large, soulful brown eyes stared back at her.

Wrangler, the massive mixed-breed dog—half Mastiff, half Retriever—rested his head on his front paws, his body poised with quiet anticipation. His tail gave a slow, rhythmic wag, rattling the bed frame ever so slightly. Seeing Maggie stir, he perked up, eyes widening with excitement. His tail thumped harder, shaking the bed a little more, and his pink tongue lolled out of his mouth in a happy pant.

Maggie smiled.

She had rescued Wrangler from an animal shelter four years ago, a decision that had changed both of their lives. The shelter had feared he would never find a home—his sheer size alone intimidated most adopters. With his broad, muscular frame and dominant Mastiff features, he looked more formidable than friendly. But Maggie had seen something else in him: a gentleness beneath the imposing exterior, a quiet loyalty waiting to be nurtured.

At the time of his adoption, the veterinarian estimated him to be just over a year old, yet he already weighed a staggering 150 pounds. Despite his size, he had never been anything but sweet. He had bonded with Maggie instantly, following her around with unwavering devotion.

Now, as she sat there, Wrangler watched her every movement, his tail still wagging in hopeful anticipation.

As Maggie stretched and moved, Wrangler followed suit, extending his front legs before shaking his entire body from head to tail. He then trotted toward her, pressing his wet nose against her cheek before swiping his pink tongue across her face. She laughed, attempting to hold him back.

Good boy. You actually let me sleep in this morning," she murmured, scratching behind his ears. Are you ready to go outside?"

At the word *outside*, Wrangler s ears perked, and his tail thumped against the bed. Maggie smiled as she rolled out of bed, slipping on her silk robe and sliding her feet into the soft slippers beside the nightstand. A cool draft met her skin, reminding her how unpredictable Texas weather could be this time of year. March had them switching between the air conditioner during the day and the heater at night, never quite settling into one season.

Their townhome, a restored colonial from the early 1900s, had captivated Maggie the moment she first stepped into its grand foyer. The high ceilings and intricate, hand-carved moldings in each room gave it a timeless charm. Oak hardwood floors stretched across the house, except in the master bath, where a broken water pipe had forced them to replace the original wood with ceramic tile.

Come on, boy. Let s go outside."

Wrangler eagerly padded after her as she made her way down the staircase, through the dining room, and into the kitchen. She opened the back door, and he bounded into the fenced yard, immediately chasing a flock of startled birds.

Maggie chuckled as she closed the door behind him, then turned to the coffee maker. One of the small perks of sleeping in was that Victor always brewed coffee before leaving for work. She poured herself a cup, inhaling the rich aroma as she walked toward the refrigerator. A note taped to the door caught her attention.

Home for lunch around 11:30. See you soon. –V

She glanced at the clock on the microwave—11:15. Smiling, she opened the fridge and pulled out a plate of leftover pork roast. There was enough to make two hearty sandwiches. She quickly assembled them, adding pickles and chips to each plate.

As she turned on the small flat-screen TV mounted on the kitchen counter, flipping through channels until she landed on the local news, her gaze drifted back to the window. Wrangler was still at play, bounding across the yard, his powerful legs kicking up patches of grass as he chased after birds that easily evaded him.

The front door clicked shut.

Maggie turned just as Victor stepped into the kitchen. Before she could say a word, he snuck up behind her, wrapping his strong arms around her waist, pulling her into his warmth.

Good morning, Sleeping Beauty," Victor said with a warm smile.

Maggie stretched and grinned. "Good morning. You should have woken me before you left—I miss you. I even made extra noise last night to wake you, but it didn't work." She leaned in eagerly, pressing a kiss to his lips.

"I'm sorry, I didn't hear a thing," he chuckled, kissing her back. "You looked so comfortable this morning, I couldn't bring myself to wake you. How'd you sleep?"

"Good." She pulled away and walked toward the refrigerator. "What do you want to drink?"

"Tea, if we have some. I only have an hour—it's a busy day." Victor sat at the kitchen table, his gaze drifting toward the television. A news anchor was reporting a murder that had taken place downtown the night before in an alley next to the Keller Building.

Maggie froze, pitcher of tea in hand. "I was there last night. It was my last dispatch before I got off... it was horrible."

Victor turned to her. "Really? What happened?"

"A woman was nearly raped. Her husband tried to save her—he was stabbed to death right in front of her." She exhaled, gripping the counter. "I felt so sorry for her."

Victor's expression darkened. "Did they catch the guy?"

"No. But they think it's the same man who's attacked other women in the area."

Without a word, Victor reached for the remote and turned off the television. He set it down and returned to his meal.

"Let's just have a peaceful lunch," he said gently.

Maggie hesitated, then nodded, pouring the tea and taking a seat beside him.

After lunch, Victor headed back to work while Maggie finished the dishes. As she wiped the counter, she heard a soft thud behind her. Turning around, she saw Wrangler standing in the doorway, a tennis ball clutched between his teeth.

She placed her hands on her hips. "I suppose you want to play now?"

Wrangler's ears perked up. He lifted his head and released the ball, letting it bounce once before it rolled toward Maggie's feet. Then he barked.

She laughed. "How about a walk instead?"

Another excited bark. His tail wagged furiously.

"Alright, alright." Maggie headed upstairs, slipping into shorts, a bra, and a T-shirt. She planned to shower and get ready for work after their walk.

When she returned downstairs, Wrangler was already at the door, waiting patiently, his blue leash dangling from his mouth.

Maggie shook her head with a smile. "You don't waste time, do you?"

She clipped the leash onto his collar, and Wrangler's tail swayed like a pendulum, eager for their next adventure.

Each afternoon before work, Maggie faithfully walked two or sometimes three miles. She loved the feeling of the sun warming her skin and the fresh air filling her lungs. Walking wasn't just exercise—it was a moment of peace, a chance to stay fit and clear her mind. It also gave her the opportunity to catch up with her neighbors, many of whom were often outside tending their lawns.

A few of the elderly residents had come to expect her daily route. They would wait eagerly to greet her, offering Wrangler affectionate pats and the occasional dog biscuit. Their walk always ended at a small park down the street, where Maggie would rest on a bench while Wrangler played with the other dogs.

Today was a perfect spring afternoon. The golden sunlight bathed the neighborhood in warmth, while a light breeze carried the crisp scent of blooming flowers. After finishing her walk and letting Wrangler enjoy his playtime, Maggie returned home with just enough time to shower and get ready for work. She placed a fresh bowl of water on the floor and kissed Wrangler's snout before heading out.

As usual, Maggie left early, even though her workplace was only a short drive away. Arriving ahead of time gave her a chance to stay updated on department issues and catch up with the previous shift. Once a week, at the start of the third shift, the paramedics gathered in the conference room for a briefing with their supervisor on new policies and procedures.

She pulled into the parking lot with plenty of time to spare, securing a good spot near the entrance. After stepping inside, she made her way to the kitchenette and poured herself a steaming cup of coffee into her sixteen-ounce travel mug. Grabbing her stethoscope and notebook from her locker, she paused for a moment in front of the hallway mirror, trying to tame her hair.

Just then, Nicole rounded the corner, dressed casually in blue jeans and a T-shirt, her younger brother Gary trailing behind.

Nicole smirked and let out a playful whistle.

Maggie rolled her eyes. "Oh, stop it! You're not being very nice. I really need a haircut." She sighed, still fussing with her hair.

Give me a minute to change, and we can get started. I stopped by the desk—we've got unit 501. Here are the keys." Nicole tossed the vehicle keys to Maggie before disappearing into the women's locker room.

Maggie caught the keys and turned to see Gary still lingering in the hallway, staring at her.

At twenty-six, Gary was the textbook definition of a lost cause. He made no effort to hide his drug addiction, cycling in and out of rehab programs for most of his adult life. About once a month, he turned up at Nicole's door, broke and needing a place to crash after running out of money for whatever halfway house he'd been staying in. Nicole, ever the supportive sister, gave him just enough to survive—but never enough to move in with her. She had learned her lesson the hard way. The last time she let him stay, he brought his drug-addicted friends into her apartment. They got high, partied, and when Gary passed out, they stole from her. That was the breaking point. Though she still helped him from a distance, she had drawn firm boundaries.

Maggie never cared for Gary. His presence unsettled her in a way she couldn't fully explain. Though she remained polite for Nicole's sake, she felt uneasy whenever she was alone with him. He reeked of stale clothes and sweat, his greasy blond hair slicked back in a failed attempt at grooming. His sunken, shadowed eyes and pale, gaunt face screamed malnourishment. And then there were his teeth—yellowed, rotting, adding to the stench of his breath.

She avoided looking directly at him as he spoke, unwilling to meet his hollow stare. It baffled her how two siblings could be so different. Nicole was responsible, hardworking, and well-liked. Gary had been given the same opportunities, yet he had thrown them all away.

Maggie checked her watch, desperate to get away. "Nice seeing you again, Gary. I better go get the unit ready. Tell Nicole I'll meet her outside."

She turned and walked down the hall, but she could still feel his eyes lingering on her.

Sure thing, buttercup," he muttered, his voice laced with something that made her skin crawl.

Maggie cringed. She couldn t imagine the kind of woman who would willingly spend time with someone like Gary.

Maggie climbed into the passenger seat of the ambulance, exhaling as she settled in. She tried to shake off the unsettling thoughts of Gary, rolling her shoulders as if that could rid her of the lingering unease. No luck. His image still clung to the edges of her mind.

A moment later, Nicole arrived, sliding behind the wheel and firing up the engine. She glanced over at Maggie with a knowing look.

Ready to get started? Do you want to take the unit and wash it? I haven t checked the back yet, but Mike and Carlos had it earlier, and you *know* what that means." Nicole raised an eyebrow.

Maggie groaned. Say no more. Let s get it cleaned up. Then we can hit the deli before they close—I ve been craving a turkey and pickle sandwich all day."

Nicole made a face. Ugh, yuck! How can you eat turkey and pickles together?"

It s good! You should try it before you knock it. Actually, you should try more new things. Live a little." Maggie smirked.

Nicole grinned. Ah, here we go. Is this a full-length lecture, or just a short course today, Professor Maggie?"

Maggie rolled her eyes. Don t be a smartass. I m just trying to help." She turned to stare out the window, stifling a yawn.

For the next hour, they worked side by side, scrubbing down the ambulance, restocking supplies, and ensuring the oxygen tanks were full. Their shifts usually started off slow, but once the clock hit six, the calls would start rolling in.

After finishing up, they made a quick stop at the deli to grab food for later. Just as they were getting back into the ambulance, a call crackled over the radio.

Unit 501, respond to an address on Durango Street near downtown."

Nicole reached over and flipped on the red and blue lights, but left the sirens off. It wasn t an emergency, but the flashing lights would still warn other drivers to stay clear.

As they pulled up in front of the address, Maggie s stomach sank.

The apartment building was a crumbling two-story wreck, its brown brick façade stained with age and neglect. Two windows on the upper level were shattered, replaced by warped plywood covered in red spray-painted graffiti. A broken gutter sagged from the roof, barely clinging on. Five cracked cement steps led to the entrance—an entrance with no door, just a gaping hole that invited anyone inside.

The tiny front yard was nothing more than an overgrown patch of weeds, littered with cigarette butts and discarded trash.

Maggie sighed, her fingers tightening around the door handle. She had a bad feeling about whatever waited for them inside.

As Maggie and Nicole opened the back of the ambulance to retrieve the stretcher, a police officer stepped out of the building.

It was Bob Mitchell.

Nice to see other people working as many hours as I am," he greeted them with a tired smile.

Never-ending challenge," Nicole replied. How s it going, Bob?"

Good—well, except for *this*." He jerked his thumb toward the building, shaking his head in frustration.

Maggie adjusted her grip on the stretcher. What are we walking into?"

Bob exhaled. Seventy-nine-year-old Hispanic female. Breathing, has a pulse, but she s in and out of consciousness. She s a real mess." His voice lingered on the word *mess*.

He continued as they made their way inside. Her neighbor called it in after noticing no one had been in or out of the apartment for a week. The old woman s son usually stops by with her medication and groceries, but the neighbor hasn t seen him lately. I have a call into the station to track him down. He ll meet you at University."

Bob glanced back at the rundown building with a grimace. Let me know if you need anything. I ll be outside keeping the neighborhood bums away from your unit."

With that, he turned and headed back toward the street.

Maggie and Nicole climbed the narrow stairwell to the second floor, their boots echoing on the worn steps. The hallway reeked of urine, the stench clinging to the air like something alive. Cockroaches darted across the matted carpet, disappearing into the cracked walls.

They left the stretcher in the hall, opting to bring only their equipment into the cramped one-bedroom apartment.

Inside, a second officer stood near the doorway, his arms crossed.

She's over here," he said, jerking his chin toward the interior. His face twisted in disgust. "If you two are good, I'm gonna wait outside. I can't take this smell."

He didn't wait for an answer. The door creaked as it swung shut behind him.

Maggie swallowed against the bile rising in her throat and exchanged a glance with Nicole.

This was going to be bad.

Maggie set her equipment bag on the floor and leaned in. "Ma'am, my name is Maggie. We're here to help you."

The frail woman on the bed didn't respond. She lay motionless beneath a small, stained quilt, her body cold and pale. Her gray hair, tangled and matted, suggested she had spent days shifting weakly from side to side—the only movement she had likely managed before exhaustion and dehydration overtook her.

Maggie inhaled sharply as a stale odor filled her nose. Gently lifting the woman's nightgown, she saw a wet stain of old urine and feces. Quickly, she lowered the fabric, hoping to contain the smell.

She glanced at Nicole, who was already checking for respirations. Maggie reached for the woman's wrist, pressing her fingers against the paper-thin skin. Nothing. Moving quickly, she placed her fingertips inside the woman's ankle, searching for a pulse. Faint but present.

As Nicole rummaged through the equipment bag, Maggie pulled out her stethoscope, listening intently to the woman's labored breathing. She retrieved a small penlight from her shirt pocket and lifted the woman's eyelid, flashing the beam across her pupils. A hazy bluish film covered her retina—cataracts had long since clouded her vision.

"Pupils are sluggish, but reactive," Maggie noted aloud.

She needs fluids," she added, though she knew Nicole was already ahead of her.

I.V. in place and running," Nicole confirmed, holding the plastic needle cap between her teeth as she secured the line.

Maggie exhaled. Let s roll her—check for bedsores."

Together, they carefully turned the woman onto her side, supporting her head as they moved. Maggie s stomach twisted. Dark bruises covered her back, and open sores seeped greenish pus, the wounds infected and untreated.

Maggie s jaw tightened. How could someone let their own mother get this bad?"

Nicole s face darkened. Her son should be shot," she muttered. Then, she noticed a single tear slipping from the woman s eye. Her expression softened.

Nicole reached for the woman s frail hand, her voice gentle. It s going to be okay. We re going to take good care of you. Don t be afraid."

Maggie took a deep breath and squared her shoulders. Let s get moving. I ll grab the cops to help with the stretcher."

A few moments later, they had the woman secured, though they knew she wouldn t—*couldn t*—move.

As they loaded the stretcher into the back of the ambulance, the rumble of an old engine caught Maggie s attention. A battered 1977 Chevy Nova pulled up behind them, its exhaust sputtering as it came to a stop.

A grungy, overweight man with greasy black hair climbed out, reeking of cigarettes and neglect. He stomped toward them, his bloodshot eyes darting between Maggie, Nicole, and the police officers.

What the hell s going on here? Where are you taking my mom?" He took a long drag off his cigarette, then flicked the still-lit butt onto the patchy, trash-littered lawn. I can t afford another damn hospital bill. Social Security barely covers the rent in this shithole."

Nicole stiffened, her hands balling into fists as she stepped forward aggressively. Before she could close the distance, Maggie intercepted, placing a firm hand against Nicole s chest.

Listen, you dirtbag—" Nicole started, her voice sharp with fury.

Before she could say more, Bob and his partner stepped in.

It s all right, Nicole," Bob said coolly. His sharp gaze settled on the man, dripping with disdain. We ll take care of this *fine model of a citizen*."

His partner let out a dry chuckle.

I m pretty sure there are a few laws covering neglect we can book him on," Bob added, grabbing the man s arm and steering him toward the squad car.

The man barely resisted, muttering curses under his breath.

Maggie turned back to Nicole and saw the fury still burning in her expression. The vein on her temple bulged, and the artery in her neck pulsed visibly. She was seething.

I ll drive," Maggie said, holding out her hand for the keys. You stay with her and cool off."

Nicole exhaled sharply, hesitating only a second before tossing Maggie the keys. Without a word, she climbed into the back of the ambulance beside their patient.

The ride to University Hospital was short. They handed off the elderly woman to the emergency room staff, finished their paperwork, and methodically cleaned the ambulance. Soon, they were ready for another call.

To pass the time, Nicole pulled into the parking lot of an elementary school next to a quiet playground. She shut off the engine and lowered the volume on the radio.

Damn, I'm still mad," she muttered, her fingers drumming against the steering wheel. I hate people like that. How can someone just *not* take care of their own mother?"

I know," Maggie replied.

The word *irresponsible* echoed in her mind, triggering an unwelcome thought of Gary.

Nicole sighed heavily. I just can't shake it. I guess I'm already in a shitty mood. Gary came stumbling in last night around two in the morning. He got into a fight at some bar—his hand was all busted up, blood all over his shirt. I had to clean him up. Again."

Maggie stayed quiet, listening.

He can't hold down a job," Nicole continued, her voice softer now, laced with exhaustion. I don't know what to do to help him anymore."

Maggie studied her friend's face, noting the hurt behind her words. Nicole truly cared for Gary, and that was something Maggie could never quite understand. But she pushed her own feelings aside, reaching deep within herself for compassion.

Listen, don't beat yourself up over his life," Maggie said gently. You've done all you can, and now you need to step aside and let fate take its course. You can't make Gary change unless he *wants* to. And honestly? If you keep picking up the pieces for him, you might be hurting him more than helping."

Nicole sighed, rubbing her temples. "Yeah, I know. I just wish it was easier."

She lifted her gaze and met Maggie's eyes, holding the moment a little too long before realizing it. Quickly, she looked away, fidgeting with the steering column—a habit Maggie had noticed before. Nicole only did that when she was nervous.

She had been in love with Maggie from the moment they met at the station two years ago. It was a quiet, unspoken love, one she had forced herself to suppress. Maggie wasn't a lesbian. She knew that. But it didn't stop her from feeling the way she did.

There had been a close call once—a fleeting moment at a New Year's Eve party after their first year working together. As the countdown reached zero, they turned toward each other, caught in the excitement of the moment. When the room erupted in cheers, Nicole kissed Maggie on the lips.

For a second, they had just stared at each other.

Nicole was sure Maggie had seen right through her then, had *felt* the truth she had spent so long hiding. She had been seconds away from saying it—three simple words that carried the weight of her heart.

But before she could, Victor had swooped in, pulling Maggie into a celebratory kiss of his own.

They had never spoken about it again.

Nicole forced herself back to the present.

"You gonna be alright?" Maggie asked, breaking the silence. "If you need someone to talk to, Victor has a great therapist. He's been seeing him for months."

Nicole forced a chuckle. "Nah, I'll be fine. But... why does Victor see a therapist?"

Maggie hesitated. "He had some things to work through from his childhood. And when his first wife died, he just... shut down. Bottled everything up. He had a few blowups at work, so his boss basically forced him to get help. He's come a long way since then." She shrugged. "Now, he still sees his therapist, but it is more like a friendship thing. Though I think it's a pretty expensive friendship—he still pays him for every session. But I try not to pry."

They sat in the quiet of the evening, eating their dinners as the sun dipped below the horizon. The sky was streaked with deep oranges, reds, and blues, fading into the cool of the night. A soft breeze drifted in through Maggie's open window, sending a slight shiver down her spine.

The radio crackled.

A voice echoed through dispatch, rattling off a new call sign. Nicole's fingers instinctively turned up the volume as she reached for the microphone.

"Unit 4, copy," she said, acknowledging the call.

She started the engine. "Parson's Nursing Home. Chest pain. Transfer to the cardiac floor at Methodist."

Maggie exhaled, glancing at the clock. Seven o'clock. Their shift was almost over.

Nicole pulled onto the road, driving just a little slower, hoping this would be their last call of the night.

The transport of the cardiac patient to Methodist Hospital went smoothly, wrapping up an uneventful night. These were the shifts they both looked forward to—steady, predictable, free from chaos.

After cleaning out their unit and refueling, they headed back to the station. As they walked inside, Nicole casually draped an arm over Maggie's shoulder.

"Thanks for being such a good friend tonight," she said, her voice softer than usual. "I really appreciate it."

Maggie smiled. "Anytime. Get some rest."

With their shift officially over, Maggie finished her last tasks before heading out into the quiet city streets. Weeknights at this hour were calm, the roads nearly empty. She pulled her BMW into the garage, parking beside Victor's little red pickup.

Inside, she moved through the house on autopilot—routine guiding her steps. She ran a hot bath, letting the warmth ease the tension from her body before slipping into her pajamas.

Peeking into the bedroom, she saw Victor's silhouette beneath the blankets, his slow, rhythmic snoring confirming he was already asleep. At the foot of the bed, Wrangler stirred, lifting his head with a drowsy expression before stretching and trotting after her.

In the kitchen, Maggie made herself a cup of hot tea, then curled up on the couch, flipping through late-night infomercials until she found something halfway interesting. Wrangler hopped up beside her, resting his head in her lap and nudging her arm.

For a while, she simply sat there, absently stroking his fur, sipping her tea, and letting the quiet settle around her.

An hour later, she switched off the television, turned out the lights, and climbed into bed next to Victor. As she curled up against his warmth, sleep came quickly, pulling her into its embrace.

CHAPTER THREE

"As I count backward, you will continue to relax, drifting deeper and deeper into sleep. Ten... nine... sinking further and further. Eight... seven... your body is growing heavy, completely at ease. Six... five... four... you re slipping into a deep state of tranquility. My voice is the only sound you hear. Three... two... one... You are completely relaxed."

Dr. Webster spoke in a calm, measured tone to the man lying on the leather sofa.

"You may keep your eyes closed. You are traveling back in time. You are nine years old, back home in Detroit with your mother and sister on Woodward Avenue. Can you see your mother? Tell me what you see, Victor."

Seated in a tan leather chair angled for an unobstructed view of his client, Dr. Webster observed Victor closely. The dimly lit office allowed only a sliver of sunlight to filter through the vertical blinds covering the two large windows. Over time, Dr. Webster had grown accustomed to the subdued lighting as he transcribed notes during sessions. His notebook rested on the chair s arm, his elbow propped against the opposite side. An expensive silver-and-gold pen hovered near his lips, tapping lightly against them as he listened intently to Victor s response.

"Yes, I can see her. She and Emma are putting groceries away. Mom s in a hurry."

Victor kept his eyes closed, visualizing the scene, a faint smile appearing on his lips.

"Continue," Dr. Webster urged gently.

"Emma s crying. Mom s running late—she s leaving for work. She kisses me on the cheek before she goes and tells me to be a good boy for Uncle Bob."

Victor s breathing grew shallow, and he hesitated.

"Victor, concentrate. Slow your breathing. Keep going."

"We ate dinner. Uncle Bob made hot dogs and beans."

Victor s smile returned, his eyelids fluttering slightly as he spoke. But then, the mood shifted.

"Then he made us play some games. I told him I didn t like playing his games anymore... but he got really mad."

Sweat gathered on Victor s forehead. His voice faltered. The once-calming memory took a sudden turn.

"No... I don t want to play!" Victor yelled, his fists clenching. "Uncle Bob is really mad. He said he has to punish Emma because I was bad."

Tears slipped down his cheeks as his body tensed, fists still tightly closed, his eyes sealed shut as if shielding himself from the past.

"I was a bad boy. I told him I d be good... begged him not to hurt Emma. But he wouldn t listen. He said if I told anyone, he d hurt her even more."

Victor's breath came in short, sharp gasps.

"Victor, listen to my voice," Dr. Webster said firmly but calmly. "You are waking up. You re coming back now."

Victor's eyes fluttered open. He shifted upright, wiping away a tear before coughing as he struggled to steady his breath. Dr. Webster handed him a glass of water.

"Thank you." Victor downed the entire glass.

"Are you all right? You were close. One day, you ll understand—it wasn t your fault. But you're still blocking out the past. Let s hold off on the hypnosis for now and just talk. How are you feeling?"

"I'm alright."

Victor leaned back against the Italian leather sofa, lacing his hands behind his head. He ran his palms over his scalp and down his face.

Dr. Webster wasn t convinced. He smirked slightly. "You're not getting off the hook that easily. You know how this works—you pay me, I listen, and you talk. So, no more short answers. Let s try again. How are you *really* feeling?"

He walked over to the window, tugging at the vertical blinds to let more sunlight spill into the dim office. Then, he picked up an exquisitely hand-carved wooden pipe, placed the thin mouthpiece between his lips, and flicked his lighter, igniting the tobacco. Inhaling deeply, he let the smoke swirl in his lungs before exhaling in a slow, white cloud. Removing his thick-framed glasses, he turned his gaze back to Victor, scrutinizing him.

"Go on. I m waiting," the doctor pressed.

"Really, I m fine," Victor muttered, avoiding eye contact.

Dr. Webster leaned against his desk. "Let s talk about your uncle. Tell me what you remember about him."

A shadow crossed Victor's face. A memory flickered to life—a large figure looming over a small, struggling girl. Her legs kicked frantically, desperate to break free from the crushing weight. The image vanished as quickly as it came. Victor shook his head, dragging his hands over his face, then hunched forward, elbows on his knees.

"What's wrong? Tell me what you remember," Dr. Webster pressed.

"Nothing. I really need to go. I'll see you next week."

Victor stood abruptly, heading straight for the door before the doctor could stop him. As the door shut behind him, Dr. Webster sighed, took another slow puff from his pipe, and scratched his head. He lowered himself into his chair, exhaling as he opened the thick chart labeled *Victor Reed*.

Just outside the office, Victor halted. His hand curled into a fist, and he brought it hard against his forehead.

"Quit," he muttered under his breath. He struck his head again, as if trying to knock loose the thoughts clawing at his mind. The hallway was empty—only his own voice echoed back at him.

Glancing at his watch, he realized it was already five o'clock. *Maggie's night off.* He had promised her dinner—and maybe a movie. Shoving the thoughts aside, he hurried out of the building. When Victor arrived home, the smell of simmering sauce and fresh herbs greeted him. Maggie was in the kitchen, moving between the stove and the counter, her back to him. He set his briefcase down on the table and leaned in, pressing a kiss to her cheek.

"Hey there, beautiful. I thought we were going out for dinner." He reached down to pet Wrangler, their dog, as he spoke.

Maggie glanced over her shoulder. "I figured a nice, quiet dinner at home sounded better. You're late—busy day?"

Before he could answer, she wrinkled her nose and took a step back.

"Never mind. You must have been with Dr. Webster." She fanned the air in front of her face. "I can *smell* that awful pipe tobacco. How do you stand that?"

Victor chuckled. "It's not so bad. You get used to it."

Shaking his head, he loosened his tie. "I'm gonna go wash up. How long do I have?"

"About five minutes." Maggie wiped her hands on a kitchen towel, then opened the refrigerator. "Take your time—it's pasta. It'll keep."

Victor returned downstairs, his damp hair neatly combed in place. A subtle trace of cologne lingered as he took his seat at the small wooden table. Maggie brought over a pan and poured the rich, red sauce onto his pasta.

"Did you still want to go out tonight?" he asked, breaking off a piece of garlic bread and tossing it to Wrangler, who caught it eagerly.

Maggie settled into the chair across from him, placing a napkin on her lap. "No... do you mind if we just stay in? I'm tired, and I feel like I haven't seen you all week. I want you all to myself. We can cuddle on the couch and watch a movie?"

Victor smiled. "Sounds perfect to me."

After dinner, they cleaned the kitchen, restoring everything to order. Maggie moved into the family room, lighting a few candles, their soft glow casting flickering shadows against the walls. Victor followed, carrying a glass of red wine in one hand. He picked up the remote to turn on the television, but before he could press a button, Maggie leaned in, her lips meeting his in a slow, lingering kiss.

He set the remote aside, wrapping his arms around her waist as she pressed closer. As he leaned back into the soft leather couch, she climbed onto his lap, draping a cozy blanket over her back. His hands roamed gently along her sides, feeling the warmth of her body against his. Their kisses deepened, growing more intense by the second. Victor's fingers traced the hem of her knit skirt, inching it up past her waist. With practiced ease, he slipped off her silk panties. Maggie's fingers found his belt, unbuckling it with deliberate urgency. As she unzipped his trousers, they continued to explore each other, lost in the moment.

"I've waited for this all day," Maggie whispered into Victor's ear, her breath warm against his skin. A shiver ran through him as she reached down, her fingers brushing against his growing arousal.

With a low groan, Victor rolled on top of her, his lips trailing down her neck, his tongue gliding over her collarbone. He pulled her shirt down, exposing her breast, and took her nipple into his mouth, sucking deeply. Maggie gasped, arching against him, her body responding to his touch. His hand slipped between her thighs, feeling the wet heat that signaled her desire.

Victor took his time, savoring every reaction, teasing her mercilessly. He moved inside her, only to stop just as she pushed against him, silently pleading for more. Each time she neared the edge, he slowed, keeping her right at the brink of release. He relished the control, the way she writhed beneath him, desperate for him to let her go over the edge.

Their passion lasted deep into the night, their bodies entangled until exhaustion finally claimed them. As Victor dozed off, Maggie remained in his arms, her fingers absently tracing patterns along his skin. The television flickered in the dimly lit room, catching her attention.

The *11 o clock news* broadcast a live report from a crime scene. Maggie immediately recognized Detective Mallory, the lead investigator, as he gave a statement to the press. Her stomach tightened as she recalled the brutal attacks on multiple women. The victims had been beaten and raped with unspeakable cruelty. The most recent survivor had lost her husband, but at least the attacker hadn t finished what he had intended with her.

Maggie exhaled slowly, her mind drifting back to her college days. Before becoming a paramedic, she had studied criminal justice, taking courses that delved into the psychology of serial rapists. She still remembered the unease those lessons had stirred in her. That fear had led her to volunteer as a rape counselor—an experience that, in turn, guided her toward the medical field. Helping victims heal had felt more meaningful than chasing the criminals.

Maggie turned away from the television and let her gaze settle on Victor as he slept. Her eyes traced the contours of his face, as if memorizing every line and shadow. Slowly, she lifted her index finger and brushed it lightly across his lips, her touch barely there.

Victor stirred, licking his lips in his sleep. She continued the delicate motion until his eyelids fluttered open.

Hey," he murmured, stretching his arms. I must have dozed off." He lifted his head to glance at the clock, blinking away the last remnants of sleep.

Let s go to bed," Maggie whispered, rising to her feet.

Okay," he yawned, pushing himself up.

Maggie moved through the room, extinguishing the candles one by one, their soft glow fading into darkness. Victor turned off the television, and Wrangler, ever loyal, padded after them as they made their way upstairs.

CHAPTER FOUR

Maggie's workweek was beginning just as Victor's weekend started. The past two days of beautiful weather made it even harder for her to shift back into work mode. That morning, she and Victor lingered in bed longer than usual, savoring a rare, unhurried moment together. Eventually, they managed to roll out of bed and start their day.

Victor had plans to play golf with a client from the brokerage firm in the early afternoon, while Maggie needed to stop by the pet store to pick up dog food for Wrangler before heading to work. Rather than eating at home, they decided to take separate cars, have lunch together, and then go their own ways.

After their meal and her quick stop at the store, Maggie still had time before her shift. Instead of waiting, she chose to head in early to complete her peer review for the week. As part of the team, each paramedic was responsible for reviewing one colleague's patient chart. If her shift was slow, she typically used that downtime to handle paperwork, but sometimes she preferred getting it done beforehand.

When she arrived at the station, she finished the review just before her partner, Nicole, showed up. Grabbing the keys to the ambulance, Maggie stepped outside, preparing for the long night ahead.

Nicole arrived as Maggie was in the back of the unit, cleaning and organizing supplies in preparation for their shift.

Nicole leaned casually against the back of the ambulance, a smirk playing on her lips. "Well, look at this... I should be late more often."

Maggie glanced over her shoulder while organizing the equipment bins. "Bad traffic?" she asked, counting supplies.

"No, it's Gary again," Nicole sighed. "He showed up just as I was leaving for work—needed a place to stay tonight. I came this close to saying no." She held up her fingers, barely an inch apart.

Maggie raised an eyebrow. "But?"

Nicole exhaled, shaking her head. "But I keep seeing that helpless little boy when I look in his eyes. I don't know, Mags. Maybe my mom should've done more for him. Maybe she did all she could. I just have a hard time turning my back on him."

Maggie gave her a sympathetic look. "I don't know what to tell you. Just be careful, okay? You ready to get started?"

Before Nicole could respond, the dispatch radio crackled to life: "Unit 499, respond."

That was their call. Nicole walked around to the front seat, grabbing the microphone. "Unit 499, copy," she confirmed.

The call sent them to a residential area just a few miles from Maggie's house. A bedridden woman in her late forties had dialed 911, reporting that some young boys had broken into her home.

As they arrived on the scene, Officer Matt Coronado from the San Antonio Police Department was already waiting for them. He greeted them with a knowing smile.

"Hey, Nicole. Too bad you got stuck with this one."

39

Nicole smirked. "Hey, Matt."

Maggie waved from the back of the ambulance. "What are we dealing with?"

Matt shook his head, still smiling. "You're gonna need at least two of those," he said, nodding toward the stretcher.

Nicole frowned. "What do you mean?"

Matt sighed. "It's Miss Jackson. Her medical problem? Severe—severe—obesity. I'd say she's at least 500 pounds. Lives alone, calls in for food and medicine, then just tosses everything on the floor when she's done. The place smells awful."

Maggie wrinkled her nose. "That bad? You should have asked for the bariatric unit, that could have saved time. Don't go anywhere."

"Oh, it gets worse," Matt continued. "She's got a hole in the mattress where she—well, you get the picture. A pan underneath catches everything. It's bad. Really bad."

"Why does she need to go to the hospital?" Maggie asked, adjusting the strap on her bag.

Matt sighed. "Some teenage boys broke in, wearing ski masks. They mostly just trashed the place—knocked over her TV, broke a lamp, called her names, and scared the hell out of her. We think it was someone from one of the delivery services. She says she's having chest pain, so... lucky you." He smirked as they walked toward the house.

Nicole shot him a look. "Do me a favor and call dispatch for the bariatric unit to meet us here, and don't go anywhere we will need some muscle here."

"Yeah, yeah," he muttered, leading them inside.

Since Miss Jackson couldn t move much, she had turned her living room into a bedroom. As soon as they stepped through the door, a massive Black woman with pink curlers and matted hair was mid-rant, hurling obscenities at the two officers standing near the wreckage of her belongings.

Matt hadn t exaggerated, she was easily over 500 pounds, sitting in the middle of a custom-made bed angled at 45 degrees, likely the only position she could tolerate. Her arms and head were the only parts of her body she seemed able to move. She waved a paper Chinese fan dramatically, fanning herself between outbursts.

Well, it s about damn time! A person could die waiting for an ambulance in this town!" Her sharp eyes flicked between Nicole and Maggie before returning to the officers. And you two—get the hell out of here! You re making a mess of my things."

She flung her arms up, sending the rolls of skin beneath them into motion, then dropped them back down with a loud sigh, as if the simple act of moving was exhausting.

Maggie suppressed a grimace as she stepped forward. The stench hit her first—stale sweat, rotting food, and something far worse. She bent slightly, stealing a glance beneath the bed, and immediately regretted it. Just as Matt had warned, a rusted pan sat underneath, catching whatever waste the woman couldn t be bothered to dispose of properly.

Bracing herself, Maggie carefully navigated over empty food containers and trash as she approached the bedside.

Miss Jackson, I m Maggie, and this is Nicole. We need to examine you. Are you still experiencing chest pain?"

The woman sighed, controlling her tone for the first time. Feels like my heart s gonna pound outta my chest. My arms are tingling, too."

Do you have a history of chest pain?"

No, just high blood pressure. But those bastard kids—I swear, I m getting me a gun. Just let them try to come in here again."

She grumbled while Maggie continued her assessment, starting from the head down, removing her stethoscope from her neck she listen to breath sounds and checking blood pressure. Meanwhile, Nicole examined the lower half, pressing gently on Miss Jackson s swollen feet and moving up to check her femoral pulse.

Finding it weak, Nicole carefully lifted the woman s gown just enough to expose her upper thigh. But the thick layers of adipose tissue made it nearly impossible to locate a pulse. She tried pulling apart a skin fold to get a better angle, and the moment she did, a nauseating stench filled the air.

Then she saw movement.

Something writhed in the damp crevices of Miss Jackson s skin.

Maggie, take a look at this," Nicole said, keeping her voice steady.

Maggie stepped around the bed, her eyes narrowing as she leaned in. Miss Jackson grunted, straining to lift her body.

What? What is it? Is something wrong?" she asked, her tone shifting to panic.

Nicole pulled the skin apart just enough for Maggie to see what lay beneath.

Maggots.

Clusters of wriggling white larvae burrowed into decaying flesh, feasting on the rotting tissue. The smell of infection—putrid, overwhelming—rose like a physical force.

Maggie's stomach lurched.

She clamped a hand over her mouth and stumbled back, throat burning.

"Oh...oh, I'll be right back. Excuse me," she gasped, rushing for the door.

As she staggered outside, gulping fresh air, she could still hear Miss Jackson's frantic voice echoing behind her.

"What is it? What's wrong? Tell me!"

"Miss Jackson, can you move your legs for me?" Nicole asked gently.

The woman strained, her face twisting with effort as she barely shifted her knees. The movement was small, but it was something.

"Good, very good," Nicole encouraged. "My partner went to get the stretcher. It looks like some food or crumbs may have dropped on the bed, and some maggots have taken up residence in the folds of your skin. We need to get you to the hospital so they can clean you up properly. You'll likely need antibiotics, but the most important thing is getting you to the ER."

She reached out and gave Miss Jackson's hand a reassuring squeeze.

The woman's expression changed. Tears welled in her eyes, her bravado slipping away.

"Maggots?" she whispered. "Are you sure? I can't feel anything."

Nicole nodded. "I'm sure. But don't worry—we'll get you the care you need. You're not alone in this."

Just then, Maggie returned as the bariatric unit arrived to assist with transport. Nicole glanced up, checking her partner's face. Maggie gave a small nod—she was ready.

With the help of several officers, the specialized team carefully maneuvered Miss Jackson onto the reinforced stretcher. They worked together to ensure her comfort and stability, securing her as gently as possible. Maggie held her breath, silently praying the equipment would support the weight. It groaned under the pressure but held firm.

As they wheeled Miss Jackson out, the night air did little to clear the unsettling sensation lingering in Maggie's stomach.

After safely transporting Miss Jackson to the emergency room at University Hospital, Maggie and Nicole decided to hold off on lunch. The image of the maggots left an unpleasant weight in Maggie's chest.

They spent the next half-hour scrubbing down the ambulance and refueling before their next call. The rest of the shift was mercifully uneventful—just a few transport calls between a nursing home and the hospital, plus one family dispute.

By the time they returned to the station at exactly eleven o'clock, exhaustion had settled in.

"Have a good night. See you tomorrow," Nicole called out, heading for her black Ford Explorer.

Maggie waved, watching her go before turning toward the building.

Nicole lived in a refurbished Victorian-style home on Broadway Street, close to downtown. The house had been divided into four apartment units, and she occupied one of the larger ones upstairs. The rent was cheap, the accommodations modest, but the property was clean and well-maintained by its owner, Marco Rodriguez.

Marco, a divorced man in his late forties, owned several old houses along Broadway Street and made his living renting out apartments. He handled all the maintenance himself, from plumbing repairs to lawn care. After learning the hard way with unreliable tenants, he had become selective, renting only to those he believed were responsible enough to pay on time and take care of the space.

Nicole's neighbors included an older widower, who lived below her with her two dogs, and a young, newly married couple in the other downstairs unit. The apartment across from Nicole's was vacant.

The widow, a retired schoolteacher, had become like a second mother to Nicole over the years. She had no living family, which made their bond even stronger. Her late husband had called her Minnie, a nickname that stuck. When her husband passed five years ago, she could no longer keep up with homeownership and moved into the apartment at the same time Nicole did.

Their friendship was mutually beneficial. Nicole ran errands for Minnie and took her grocery shopping since she no longer drove, and in return, Minnie cooked meals and even packed lunches for her to take to work.

Tonight, as Nicole pulled into the driveway after her shift, she noticed Minnie pacing the front porch. She wore her pajamas beneath a long housecoat, slippers on her feet, and her gray hair was set in curlers beneath a nylon scarf.

The moment Nicole stepped out of her car, Minnie rushed toward her.

"Is something wrong, Minnie?" Nicole asked, picking up her pace.

Minnie's hands trembled as she clutched her housecoat. "Yes! I'm so glad you're home. I waited—I knew you'd be here soon," she said nervously.

As Nicole reached the porch, loud voices echoed from upstairs, followed by a sharp scream.

"It's your brother, Gary. He brought a woman home with him. They've been fighting for almost half an hour," Minnie explained.

Nicole sighed, frustration mixing with concern. "I'm sorry, Minnie. Go back inside—I'll handle it. Don't worry."

She gently wrapped an arm around Minnie, escorting her inside. Nicole waited until she heard the click of the deadbolt before turning and sprinting up the stairs.

Flinging open her apartment door, she froze at the sight before her.

Gary was on top of a woman, pinning her arms over her head. Her clothes were torn, exposing her bare skin. He swung his arm toward her face.

Nicole reacted instantly. She grabbed his arm and yanked him off.

The woman curled into a ball on the floor, sobbing. Nicole shoved Gary hard against the wall, her pulse pounding.

"What the hell are you doing? Are you crazy?" she yelled.

Gary sneered, his words slurring. "She wants more money. The bitch."

Nicole's stomach churned. "I'm done with you, Gary. This is it."

"What are you mad at me for? She's just a lousy whore."

Nicole clenched her fists. "Get out. Don't come back. I've had enough."

She shoved him toward the door and followed, watching as he stumbled down the stairs. He kicked over the garbage cans, sending metal lids clattering across the yard. The front door slammed behind him.

Nicole lingered at the top of the stairs, waiting, heart hammering in her chest. Only when the sounds of his angry departure faded did she exhale and step back inside.

The woman was still curled up on the floor, shaking. She was young and painfully thin, with long black hair and too much makeup smudged on her delicate face. Nicole knew the type—many prostitutes worked the streets of Broadway, hoping to attract business from the military men at Fort Sam Houston.

"Are you alright?" Nicole asked softly, reaching out.

The young woman flinched.

Nicole held up her hands in a calming gesture. "I'm not going to hurt you. I'm a paramedic—I just want to check your injuries, okay?"

She gently brushed back the girl's long black hair, revealing a swollen black eye, a welt above her brow, and a thin cut near the corner of her lip. The girl clutched her torn shirt around her shoulders, trying to cover herself.

Nicole exhaled and stood. "Hang on, I'll get you something to wear."

She disappeared into her bedroom and returned with a red flannel button-up.

"It's not fancy, but it'll keep you warm," she said, draping it over the girl's shoulders.

The woman hesitated before pulling it on, buttoning it up with shaky hands.

Nicole rummaged through the kitchen, returning with antiseptic and bandages. She poured the solution onto a cotton pad and dabbed at the girl's injuries.

"I'm really sorry about what he did to you. There's no excuse for it."

The girl scoffed, wincing slightly. "It's not your fault he's a maniac. Pervert asshole."

She touched the bandage Nicole had placed near her eyebrow, then glanced up, her expression shifting. "You know..." she said, trailing her fingers over Nicole's hand. "I can return the shirt another night... and maybe—" her voice dropped into something playful "—I could do a little something for you. I swing both ways, baby."

Nicole sighed inwardly. It didn't take long for the young woman to start working again.

She forced a small smile and shook her head. "No, it's okay. Please, keep the shirt. Your eye will be black for a while, but otherwise, I think you'll be alright."

She reached for her wallet, pulled out seventy-five dollars, and pressed it into the girl's palm as they walked to the door.

"I hope this helps. Do you need a ride somewhere? Anyone I can call for you?"

The woman smirked, slipping the cash into her purse. "No, honey... but if you change your pretty little mind, you know where to find me."

She started down the steps, but Nicole hesitated.

"Listen," she called after her. "Do you have a place to go? Somewhere off the streets? I might be able to help you get a job or something."

The girl stopped mid-step, hesitated for a moment, then turned to face Nicole.

"I m sure you mean well. You seem really nice," she said, offering a small, knowing smile. "But don t worry about me. You should get your brother some help, though."

She cocked her head slightly before turning and walking away.

Nicole hesitated. "Hey, one last question—do you know Gary, or did he just pick you up?"

The girl paused but didn t look back. "I ve seen him around the streets, but I don t know him well. He said he had what I needed. Money..."

Her voice trailed off as she disappeared into the darkness.

Nicole lingered in the doorway for a moment, staring after her, then exhaled and stepped back inside. The room was a mess—empty beer cans littered the floor, remnants of Gary s presence still scattered around. She bent down, picking them up one by one, the rhythmic clinking the only sound in the apartment.

With a heavy sigh, she slumped onto the couch, running both hands through her jet-black hair. Her body ached—not just from work, but from everything. The weight of it all pressed down on her, exhaustion settling in like an old friend.

She wasn t angry. Not really. Just tired. And sad.

She let her head fall back against the cushions, closed her eyes, and let sleep take her.

CHAPTER FIVE

A two-story white Victorian sat curbside along the busy stretch of Broadway. The neighborhood was a lively mix—stores, restaurants, museums, and a Catholic college all nestled together. Amidst the city's energy, this was home to Nicole.

From the moment she left her parents' house in Dallas and arrived in Alamo City, she had fallen in love with this part of town. Breckenridge Park was just a few blocks away, offering her a peaceful jogging path through the trees. San Antonio was smaller than Dallas, yet it had all the appeal of a big city, with the added charm of a close-knit community. Even longtime residents couldn't help but feel the touristy magic of walking along the river snaking below downtown's streets.

An hour's drive in any direction led to a different adventure—the ocean, dude ranches, the Hill Country, or even Mexico.

Nicole woke early, as usual.

Even when she tried to stay in bed past eight, her internal clock refused to let her sleep. As a child, she had never needed much rest—four hours was often enough to keep her going.

She sat in her living room, shifting uncomfortably on the couch. She hadn't even made it to bed last night.

The memories from the night before pressed heavily on her. She wished it had all been a dream, but she knew it had been painfully real.

Gary had betrayed her trust. Again.

He had put her in another impossible situation, forcing her to clean up his mess.

Anger tightened in her chest, but beneath it, a small part of her still hoped her younger brother was safe. No matter what he had done, she couldn't just stop caring.

Since childhood, she and Gary had always stuck together. Growing up in the streets of Dallas, they had only ever had each other.

Their parents' marriage had collapsed when Nicole was just six years old. One morning, their father walked out the door and never came back.

Their mother had no choice but to work two jobs, struggling to make ends meet. Rent, food, bills, it was a constant battle. More often than not, Nicole and Gary had been left home alone.

And even with two jobs, their mother's income had never been enough.

From as far back as Nicole could remember, she had watched over Gary. She had tried to keep him out of trouble.

But trouble had a way of finding him.

He had always struggled in school, his learning disability making it hard for him to keep up with the other kids. Frustrated and falling behind, he started skipping class.

Gary's trouble had started small.

Skipping school. Shoplifting from local stores. Petty things.

But over time, it escalated. Fights in the street. A growing temper. And then... worse.

When Gary began hurting neighborhood animals...cats, dogs, Nicole knew something was deeply wrong. But she never could understand why he carried so much anger.

And maybe she didn t want to.

Instead of facing the truth, she told herself it wasn t that bad.

She covered for him, taking the blame for things she hadn t done. She made excuses. She kept hoping, praying, that one day, Gary would just... grow out of it.

A loud thump pulled Nicole back to the present.

She blinked, sitting up on the couch. Had she imagined it?

Another two thumps echoed from below, this time, louder.

Nicole smirked and stomped her foot in response.

Minnie.

It was their unspoken code, Minnie s way of inviting her down for coffee.

Nicole rubbed her hands over her face, still feeling the weight of exhaustion from the night before. She hadn t even changed out of her uniform.

With a sigh, she got up, walked into the bedroom, and opened her nightstand drawer.

Inside was an envelope—three twenty-dollar bills tucked neatly inside.

She pulled one out, folded it, and slipped it into her pocket.

Breakfast first.

Crossing the street, she stopped at the local taco stand, ordering six breakfast tacos to go. Then, bag in hand, she walked back across and let herself into Minnie's apartment.

The door was unlocked, as always.

As Nicole stepped inside, Minnie appeared—a small ceramic coffee pot in one hand, two cups, creamer, and sugar balanced on a silver tray.

Faithfully at her heels, her two Cocker Spaniels, Bonnie and Clyde, pranced into the room.

"Here we are," Minnie said with a smile, setting the tray on the table. "Hot coffee for you, and a cup of tea for me."

Nicole took a seat on the couch, just as Bonnie and Clyde trotted over.

Wagging their tails, they pressed against her legs, demanding attention.

"I brought some tacos this morning," Nicole said, pulling them from the bag and setting them on the tray beside the coffeepot. "Hope you're hungry."

Minnie's eyes warmed as she reached for her teacup. "You know I never turn down tacos, sweetheart." But her voice softened with concern. "Everything all right from last night? Did anyone get hurt?"

Nicole sighed, unwrapping a taco. "Nothing too bad. Just a few bumps and bruises." She hesitated before adding, "I'm sorry for disturbing you. Gary is just... out of control again."

Minnie gave a knowing nod, cradling her cup. "Oh, it'll be all right, sweetie. I'm just glad no one was seriously hurt." A pause. "But I have to admit... he does frighten me sometimes."

Nicole took another bite, chewing slowly. "I just don't know what else to do for him."

Minnie set her cup down gently. "Be patient, my dear." Then, after a beat, "But be cautious."

Nicole studied her for a moment. She had never asked Minnie's age, but she guessed the older woman was around sixty. Short and plump, with wavy gray hair and deep brown eyes, Minnie carried herself with an effortless warmth—but also wisdom.

Nicole finished her taco and stood. "Sorry to eat and run. I want to get a quick jog in while the weather's nice." She leaned down, pressing a quick kiss to Minnie's cheek. "Thanks for the coffee."

Minnie smiled. "Stop by on your way to work, I'll have a little snack for you to take."

Back at her apartment, Nicole changed into shorts and a T-shirt. Stepping outside, she placed one foot on the porch steps, stretching her legs before heading out.

Her jog through the park was refreshing, the air crisp, the city just waking up. She followed the familiar path, weaving back down Broadway, until she reached home.

Stopping by the curbside mailbox, she grabbed yesterday's mail and stepped inside. A quick glance at the clock told her she still had plenty of time—enough to wash her car and shower before work.

Nicole actually enjoyed her job, something few of her friends could say.

There was deep satisfaction in helping others, in knowing that, at any moment, her presence could mean the difference between life and death.

And if that wasn't enough motivation to head into work every day...

Well, there was also Maggie...

What began as any other work day for Nicole quickly turned disastrous, four hours into her shift.

"Unit 499, respond."

Maggie reached for the handset, acknowledging the call. It had been a relentless afternoon, and they'd already handled multiple emergencies.

She flipped the siren and lights, weaving through downtown traffic.

By the time they reached the scene, the sun had nearly disappeared, casting a bluish-black hue across the sky, streaked with dying embers of orange. A police officer stood in the middle of the street, waving them forward with his flashlight.

Maggie pulled the ambulance into the narrow alleyway. Before she could even open the door, a uniformed officer approached. She rolled down the window on the passenger's side.

"Hold off on your equipment." His voice was flat, routine. "She's already dead. We just need you here for protocol. Coroners on the way."

Maggie exhaled, letting her hand drop from the door handle. "What happened?"

"Prostitute. Beaten. Probably raped." He motioned toward the alley. "Take a look if you want—just don't touch anything."

Maggie shook her head. "No thanks. I'll pass on seeing a dead prostitute." She leaned back in her seat, rolling the window back up.

Nicole, however, decided to go see what had transpired. She exited the ambulance and followed the officer.

At the end of the alley, a naked woman lay sprawled on the pavement, her skin deathly pale against the cold concrete.

Nicole's breath caught in her throat.

Her stomach clenched. Her heart pounded.

She knew this woman.

The same woman who had been in her apartment last night.

She staggered back, her pulse roaring in her ears.

The officer frowned. "You okay?"

Nicole inhaled sharply. "Yeah. I've... I've seen her before. Around Broadway."

She forced her gaze away, scanning the crime scene, searching for something—anything—familiar.

"Where is the flannel shirt I gave her?" She thought to herself.

"Do you have any suspects?" She managed to ask.

The officer shrugged. "A drunk digging through trash said he saw a white guy—blonde hair—leaving the alley. But he also mentioned a hooded figure, so we're not sure if he means one guy or two." He sighed. "Not exactly a reliable witness. Just another drunk."

Nicole's mind raced as fast as her pulse.

Tell the police? Stay silent?

Her thoughts swirled aimlessly. If she mentioned the fight between Gary and the girl, they'd immediately suspect him.

She swallowed hard.

No.

Instead, she turned and walked back to the ambulance.

Once again, her instinct to protect Gary overpowered everything else.

"Was it bad?" Maggie asked. She noticed Detective Mallory walking away from the scene.

Nicole barely registered the question. She sat frozen, staring at the officers gathered around the body.

Maggie frowned, watching her. "Hey, what's wrong?" She touched Nicole's arm.

Nicole flinched. "Nothing. It's nothing." But her eyes remained locked on the crime scene.

Maggie wasn't buying it. "No, something's up. Did you know her?"

A long pause.

Nicole met Maggie's gaze, weighing the risk of telling her the truth.

Could she trust her?

Maggie's expression softened. "You can tell me. I promise."

Nicole exhaled shakily. She broke.

She told Maggie everything—the fight, the girl, Gary, and how the woman in the alley had been in her apartment just last night.

Maggie's reaction was immediate. "You need to tell the police."

No!" Nicole's voice came out sharper than intended. She clenched the steering wheel, pressing her forehead against her hands. "I shouldn't have told you."

Maggie hesitated, then softened. "No, I'm sorry. I'm glad you did. And I won't say anything."

She squeezed Nicole's hand. "But I'm worried about you. And I'm scared for Gary."

Nicole's breath hitched.

"Do you think he did this?" Maggie asked gently.

Nicole's head shot up. "Absolutely not! Gary's not a murderer." Her voice cracked, emotion breaking through. "He may be a lot of things... but not this."

Tears burned in her gray eyes. Maggie saw the raw pain there and believed her.

She exhaled. "Then you need to find him. Fast."

At that moment, the coroner arrived.

Maggie gave Nicole's hand one last squeeze. "Come on. Let's head back. Maybe we can leave early."

They cleaned the unit quickly, returning to the station. Their supervisor approved an early departure.

As Nicole grabbed her keys, Maggie spoke up. "Do you want me to come with you?"

Nicole hesitated. For a split second, she wanted to say yes. But this was her mess. Her family.

She shook her head. "No, thanks. I think I know where he is."

Maggie nodded. "Be careful."

Nicole rushed out the door.

With nowhere else to go but home, Maggie decided to surprise Victor by coming home early and spending time with him before he went to bed.

But when she opened the garage door, his red pickup truck was missing.

She frowned, pulling her BMW into the garage.

Just as she shut off the engine, headlights flashed across the driveway.

Victor was just getting home.

As he stepped out of the truck, she leaned against her car, arms crossed. "You're out late."

Victor smirked. "You're home early."

She walked toward him. "Not happy to see your hardworking, beautiful wife?"

He laughed, but as she reached up to kiss him, she hesitated. His skin was damp with sweat.

She wrinkled her nose playfully. "You need a shower."

He chuckled. "Met Ben at the basketball court. One-on-one. Figured I'd get some cardio in."

"Mmm. So that's your excuse. What's mine?"

He gave her a look. "That's what I'm wondering. Everything okay?"

She nodded. "Nicole had some personal stuff to deal with, so we ended the shift early. I thought I'd surprise you."

Victor's grin softened. "You did."

They walked inside together.

While Victor showered, Maggie took Wrangler outside, tossing the ball across the yard. The dog's excited barks echoed in the night air.

Later, when she slipped into bed beside Victor, he wrapped an arm around her waist.

"Feels good to be home with you," she murmured against his lips.

He reached over, flipping off the light.

"Goodnight, Maggie."

CHAPTER SIX

"Sorry to keep you waiting, Victor."

Dr. Webster strode into the room, a stack of patient charts in hand, and placed them on his desk.

Victor lay stretched across the hard leather sofa but sat up as soon as the doctor entered.

"No problem," he said with a grin. "I needed a nap anyway."

Dr. Webster didn't return the smile.

"I'm concerned about how our last session ended," he said, his tone serious. "I need you to be open with me, Victor. You have to trust that anything we discuss stays in this room. If you truly want to break through these barriers from your past, we have to build that trust."

Victor hesitated, his grin fading.

"I know," he admitted. "It's just... remembering Emma is hard. Especially that accident in the woods on our way home from school. The way my mother suffered afterward." His voice dropped. "I've blocked most of it out... but it still hurts."

Dr. Webster nodded thoughtfully.

Let's take a different approach," he said, flipping open his notebook. "I want you to think about your Uncle Bob. Tell me what you remember about him."

The room remained dimly lit, the wooden blinds drawn, blocking out the harsh daylight. Shadows pooled in the corners, giving the space a calm but heavy atmosphere.

Solid oak bookshelves lined the walls, packed with hardbound medical texts. Only a small section was left uncovered, where two large windows overlooked the street below.

The dark green, maroon, and blue paisley curtains matched the custom-built leather furniture—a sofa and an oversized chair. Nestled into each corner of the couch were two large pillows, made from the same rich, heavy fabric as the drapes.

Dr. Webster leaned forward in his chair, pen in hand, waiting.

Victor sat in silence, his lips tightening as he focused, his thoughts pulling him back to a long-buried memory. He was a boy again, standing by the lake with his younger sister, Emma, and their Uncle Bob. The sun had shimmered on the water that day, but the warmth of the scene was an illusion—this was the memory that haunted him the most.

That day, Victor's view of his uncle had shifted irreversibly. Until then, Uncle Bob had been a trusted presence, someone he admired. But what happened by the water fractured that trust forever. He remembered the terror in Emma's eyes, the helplessness he felt as their uncle raped her—and worse, how he himself had been coerced, manipulated, drawn into the horror. He was only twelve. Emma was nine. Their uncle's threats ensured their silence, twisting their fear into a prison neither of them could escape.

At first, Victor had obeyed out of sheer terror. But as time passed, the lines blurred. His uncle didn't just rule them with threats—he shaped Victor's understanding of power, of desire, of what it meant to be a man.

Emerging hormones clashed with fear, creating confusion so deep that, in his young and impressionable mind, Uncle Bob almost seemed like a mentor.

They never told their mother. They never questioned what was happening. It simply became a part of life.

Now, sitting in Dr. Webster's office, the memory faded like a shadow retreating at dawn. Victor clenched his jaw, forcing his expression into neutrality. "Tell me more about your relationship with your uncle," Dr. Webster pressed gently.

Victor exhaled slowly.

"He was my mom's older brother," he said, his voice flat. "Never married. No kids of his own. He lived in our basement and helped raise us."

Dr. Webster waited.

Victor hesitated, then continued. "My dad left when I was a baby. Uncle Bob was the only father figure we had."

A brief pause. Then, an added detail—one that seemed to slip out without thought:

"Emma had a different father."

Dr. Webster didn't react, just watched.

"Our mother never told us who he was," Victor went on. "I just remember her being pregnant. Things were hard for her back then." His voice faltered. "Uncle Bob helped a lot."

A blank stare. A slow nod.

But Victor never lifted his eyes.

Dr. Webster's pen hovered over the notebook. "What about your sister, Emma?" he asked. "Tell me about the accident."

Victor exhaled, shifting forward. His elbows rested on his knees, fingers tangled together. He fidgeted—a nervous habit, or maybe a defense mechanism.

"What can I say?" he muttered. "Emma was... beautiful." His voice softened. "She had these big, blue eyes. Blonde curls. She was about to turn eleven."

Dr. Webster remained silent, letting Victor find his way through the memory.

"We always walked home together," Victor continued. "There was a shortcut through the woods behind our house. Took thirty minutes off the trip. We'd crossed that creek a hundred times before. Always used the big rocks to get across."

He swallowed hard.

"She was messing around, acting like she was gonna fall." A slight, bitter laugh. "Then she did."

Victor's jaw tensed, and his hands stilled.

"She slipped. Hit her head. The current was strong—too strong." His voice cracked. "I ran. Tried to catch her. But I couldn't keep up." He shook his head. "She just... floated away."

Silence filled the room.

Victor clenched his hands into fists. "I ran like hell, house to house, until I found someone home. They called 911. Came back with me. But it was too late."

His words faded, as if speaking them aloud drained the last of his strength.

Dr. Webster jotted something down. "It's okay, Victor," he said gently. "You did everything you could. It was an accident. Nothing more."

Victor sat back, rubbing his palms together. His gaze flickered everywhere except Dr. Webster's face.

"Well..." He hesitated. "My mom... changed. She stopped coming home. When she did, she had a whiskey bottle in her hand." His throat bobbed as he swallowed.

"Did she blame you?" Dr. Webster asked carefully.

Victor gave a small shrug, but his expression tightened. "Maybe." He let out a bitter breath. "She withdrew. I withdrew. And Uncle Bob..." He hesitated.

Dr. Webster waited.

Victor inhaled sharply. "He stepped in."

A shadow passed over his face.

"He took me everywhere—said he wanted to keep an eye on me. Took me to work with him after school. He ran a video store." Victor gave a short, humorless laugh. "Took me a while to realize what kind of video store it was."

Dr. Webster's pen stopped.

"My mom... withered away," Victor continued. His voice was quieter now. "Until she didn't exist at all."

A heavy pause.

"She committed suicide."

The weight of those words hung in the air.

Victor finally lifted his gaze. For the first time, he met Dr. Webster's eyes.

"Excellent. Talking about the past helps, Victor. Are you ready for another hypnosis session? We may get farther today while everything is fresh on your mind."

Victor hesitated, his fingers twitching on the arm of the leather couch. "I'm sorry," he said finally. "I'm not up to it today. I'm actually not feeling well. Maybe we can end this session early?"

Dr. Webster frowned slightly. "Are you sure? Anything I can help with?"

"No, just an upset stomach." Victor stood quickly, avoiding eye contact. "I'll see you next week."

Dr. Webster exhaled, watching him go. Then he turned to his desk and picked up Victor's chart. After a brief pause, he reached for a red pen and, in large letters, scrawled:

REFUSED HYPNOSIS AGAIN.

He capped the pen with a soft *click* and closed the folder.

Victor gripped the steering wheel as he navigated the traffic on IH-410. His irritation simmered beneath the surface, bubbling closer to a full boil.

Every red light. Every slow driver.

Then a sedan—a damn beige sedan—cut into his lane without signaling.

Victor slammed his palm against the wheel. "Jesus Christ!" he barked, but the driver remained oblivious, creeping forward at a snail's pace.

His jaw clenched. He could feel his pulse hammering against his temple.

By the time he finally pulled into the driveway, his hands were shaking. He exhaled hard, steering into the garage and parking beside the black BMW. But instead of getting out, he just sat there, gripping the wheel so tightly his knuckles turned white.

His chest constricted. The air felt too thick.

His fingers fumbled at his collar, yanking the top button open, then loosening his tie. He closed his eyes, resting his forehead against the wheel, forcing himself to take deep, slow breaths.

In... out...

Gradually, the pressure in his chest eased. His heartbeat slowed.

Then—*tap, tap, tap.*

Victor jerked upright, startled. His head snapped toward the driver's side window.

Maggie stood there, peering in at him with a concerned expression.

Victor?" she asked. Are you all right?"

You scared the hell out of me. What the fuck are you doing?" he snapped.

Throwing the door open, he grabbed his briefcase from the passenger seat, yanked it out with unnecessary force, and slammed the door shut so hard the truck shook. Without waiting for a response, he stalked past her toward the house.

Maggie took a small step back, startled by the sudden outburst.

I was just checking on you," she said softly. I heard the garage door..."

But Victor was already inside.

Wrangler, their faithful dog, pranced toward him, his tail wagging in excitement.

Get out of my way, boy. Go!" Victor snapped, shoving past the dog. Wrangler whimpered and retreated to the corner.

Maggie remained outside.

She wrapped her arms around herself, rubbing them as if warding off a chill. Her breathing was slow and controlled, but inside, her emotions churned—anger, frustration, sadness—all tangled together.

I hate when he acts this way," she told herself. He comes home, treats me like shit, ignores me, and I don t deserve this. I shouldn t have to tiptoe around my own damn house."

But deep down, she knew how it would go.

They d avoid the conversation. Let the tension dissolve into silence. Go to bed without speaking. Wake up pretending it never happened.

The same cycle. Every time.

Maggie clenched her fists, then exhaled sharply, shaking her head. She nudged a loose rock with the toe of her shoe, sending it tumbling into the street.

After another moment, she turned and walked inside, closing the garage door behind her.

CHAPTER SEVEN

Nicole pulled her Ford Explorer into the gravel parking lot of San Pedro 3 Par Golf and Driving Range. The small but efficient course sat tucked among department stores and a nearby residential area, almost blending into the urban sprawl. At the far end of the greens, a patch of dense trees and a flood embankment created a hidden world—one that many overlooked.

It was a known refuge.

She had spent last night driving in circles, searching for her brother with no luck. But if Gary had nowhere else to go, this might be where he ended up. The woods provided just enough cover for those who had slipped through the cracks, offering them a place to sleep and easy access to the gourmet dumpsters of downtown restaurants.

Nicole stepped out of her SUV, locking it behind her, and started toward the brush. The air changed as she moved from concrete to dirt—hot pavement giving way to the cool, damp scent of trees and decay. The deeper she walked, the more signs of life appeared. Large cardboard boxes lay scattered like makeshift homes, some reinforced with plastic tarps. Ragged clothes hung from tree branches, drying in the morning sun. A man with matted gray hair sat slumped against a tree stump, his bare feet planted in the dirt. His shirt and shoes lay beside him, along with a pile of belongings, which he instinctively pulled closer as Nicole approached.

Her eyes caught another figure, only partially visible. A pair of dirty, bare feet stuck out from the opening of a cardboard box, unmoving.

Nicole's stomach tightened.

She stepped forward. "Excuse me—I'm looking for my brother. His name is Gary."

The old man's head twitched at the sound of her voice, but he didn't look up.

"What?" he barked, voice rough from years of wear. He dragged his possessions closer, as if she might try to steal them.

Nicole raised her hands slightly. "It's okay—I'm not here to take anything." She softened her tone but spoke louder, hoping to cut through whatever haze he was in. "Do you know a man named Gary?"

A voice cut through the stillness.

"Hey, over here."

Nicole's head snapped toward the sound. A hand waved from inside another cardboard box a few feet away. She hesitated for a second, then left the old man behind and walked toward the source.

As she approached, a young Hispanic man crawled out of the opening. His denim pants were ripped at the knees, and his faded T-shirt clung to his bony frame. His hands twitched, constantly in motion. Without a word, he shoved a cigarette between his lips, flicked a cheap plastic lighter, and took a long drag. The smoke curled above them, dissolving into the damp morning air.

"Who you lookin' for?" he asked, his feet bouncing restlessly.

Nicole kept her stance firm. "My brother, Gary. He has blonde hair—"

"Oh yeah, I know Gary." The man cut her off. "Crazy dude."

Nicole's chest tightened. "Have you seen him around?"

The man's movements sped up. His eyes darted left, then right, back toward the trail she had come from, then deeper into the woods. Another long drag from his cigarette.

Then, his gaze snapped to her wallet.

"What's it worth to you, sweetie? Ten bucks? Give me ten, and I'll tell you where he is."

Nicole let out a slow breath. She had expected this.

Keeping her expression blank, she pulled out her wallet. The man leaned in slightly, eyes scanning the bills inside as she retrieved a ten-dollar bill.

Before he could snatch it, she pulled it away.

"Tell me first."

He clicked his tongue, rolling the cigarette between his fingers. "C'mon, man. I wouldn't bum you." He jerked his head toward a massive oak tree about fifty feet away. "He's over there. That's Larry's spot, but Gary's been crashing there."

Nicole's grip loosened on the bill. She handed it over.

The man snatched it fast, stuffing it into his pocket before calling out, his voice mocking.

"Hey, Gary! You got company, man! A little sweet thing, comin' your way!"

Nicole's stomach clenched at the words, but she didn't slow her steps.

A rustling sound came from the box under the oak tree.

Then, slowly, Gary crawled out.

Gary squinted up at her, using his hand as a shield against the sunlight. His face was hollow, his once-sharp features dulled by exhaustion.

"What do you want?" he asked, his voice flat, edged with irritation.

Nicole crossed her arms. "I've been looking for you for the last twenty-four hours. Where the hell have you been?"

Gary let out a short, bitter laugh. "Oh, I must've missed the part where I started having to check in with you." His tone dripped with sarcasm.

Nicole's eyes drifted over the makeshift shelters, the cardboard walls, the scattered belongings. She swallowed hard, shaking her head.

Gary caught the look and scoffed. "What? You come all this way just to give me a damn lecture? Spare me, sis. Save your breath."

Nicole's jaw tightened, but she refused to let him push her away.

"I came to tell you about the woman you were beating up the other night."

Gary's expression didn't change.

"I already know," he muttered, holding her gaze for a moment before looking away with a cocky smirk.

Nicole's stomach churned. "How do you know?"

"Word travels fast on the streets." He leaned back against the tree, rolling a loose cigarette between his fingers. Then, his lips curled into something ugly. "What... did you think I did it?"

Nicole hesitated. "I don't know. Did you see her again after you left my house?"

Gary's face hardened.

No. I didn't see the whore again." He exhaled sharply and rolled his eyes, turning away.

Nicole's chest tightened at his words.

The disrespect, the indifference—it was too much.

You know what? I'm done." Her voice came out steady, but her hands trembled. I am not taking any more of this. Don't try to contact me. Don't bother coming around. Not until you get your damn life together."

She turned on her heel and walked away, ignoring the ache in her gut.

Nicole, wait!"

Gary's voice rang out behind her, but she didn't stop.

She kept walking. Kept her eyes forward.

The second she reached her car, she ripped open the door, climbed inside, and slammed it shut.

Her breath came fast, her chest heaving as she gripped the steering wheel.

Then, in a sudden burst of rage and heartbreak, she pounded her fists against the leather, her knuckles turning white.

Without another thought, she threw the car into reverse, her tires spinning against the pavement as she tore out of the parking lot.

Nicole pulled into the parking lot of the fitness center where she held a membership. The weight of the day pressed on her, but she pushed it aside as she stepped inside. In the locker room, she quickly changed into shorts and a tank top, tying her hair back before heading to the gym floor.

For hours, she threw herself into an intense workout, each rep, each strike, each movement serving as an outlet for the stress coiling inside her. Every time her fists connected with the punching bag, memories of betrayal surfaced—her brother s broken promises, his manipulations, the way he had always leaned on her, expecting her to clean up his messes. The anger fueled her, driving her to hit harder, push further.

Then, finally, her body gave in. She launched one last punch, and as the bag swung away, she dropped to her knees, breathless. The bag swung back toward her, and she grabbed hold of it, letting herself slide onto the padded floor. Sweat soaked her hair and clothes, but she barely noticed. Instead, she focused on her breathing, on the growing sense of relief spreading through her.

For the first time, pushing herself to the extreme didn t just offer a temporary escape—it brought clarity. She could no longer allow Gary to take advantage of her. More than just releasing anger and tension, she was releasing something far heavier: the burden of feeling responsible for him.

She had made promises to herself before, vowing to walk away, only to be pulled back into his chaos. But this time felt different. This time, the resolve sat deeper, more unshakable. She would create distance, not just physically, but emotionally. No more phone calls. No more visits. No more being the one to fix things.

By the time Nicole stepped out of the gym, freshly showered, she felt lighter. The usual sadness that had always clung to decisions about her brother was absent. In its place was something new—satisfaction.

CHAPTER EIGHT

A thick cloud of black smoke billowed above the small, compact car. Flames consumed the vehicle, their heat radiating outward as bystanders stood frozen, staring in horror. Across the intersection, another car sat at an awkward angle, its front end crumpled. The windshield bore a circular crack, obscuring the driver's side.

As the ambulance pulled up, Maggie spotted several pedestrians in hospital scrubs kneeling beside a man on the ground. The accident had occurred just miles from the medical center, an area dominated by sprawling hospital campuses. As they approached, a thought crossed Maggie's mind: *If I were ever in an accident, this would be the place to have it.* She glanced at the burning car, a knot forming in her stomach. *Please let no one be trapped inside.*

Their ambulance came to a stop just as another unit arrived. Maggie and Nicole grabbed their gear and sprinted toward the injured man lying near the flaming wreckage. The other crew rushed toward the victim in the smashed car. As Maggie approached, she noticed a young woman in scrubs clutching the man's hand.

"This is the driver of the burning car," she said, her voice steady but urgent. "He was the only occupant. He's breathing and has a pulse. He has facial burns, a large laceration on his arm, and a forehead contusion. His level of consciousness fluctuates. He doesn't remember crawling out of the car, but he knows his name and the day of the week. He's a doctor—Bill Hart."

"Thanks. Are you a nurse?" Nicole asked as she set down the equipment bag.

"No, I'm a respiratory therapist on the pediatric transport team. We work with babies, so he's a little bigger than what I'm used to." The woman exhaled sharply, still gripping Bill's hand. "A couple of us had just finished our shift and were heading to grab something to eat when we saw it happen. The other car hit him from behind at full speed. His car went up in flames within seconds. I can't believe he got out." Her voice trembled as she shook her head in disbelief.

The respiratory therapist stepped back, allowing Nicole and Maggie to take over. "Bill, we are leaving you in good hands. The paramedics are here to take care of you. Good luck," she said before moving away.

Maggie leaned in, her voice calm but firm. "Bill, can you hear me? Open your eyes." As his eyelids fluttered open, she nodded. "Very good. Can you squeeze my hand?"

Bill weakly clasped her fingers. Satisfied with his response, Maggie turned to Nicole, who was already unwrapping a clean gauze bandage to tend to the cut on his arm.

"Do you feel pain anywhere else?" Maggie asked.

"No," Bill murmured, moving his head slightly to indicate his response.

Maggie placed a steadying hand on his shoulder. "Please keep your head still. We need to put a collar on you, and the hospital will take X-rays to check for any injuries." As Nicole gently held his head in place, Maggie retrieved a cervical collar from her bag and secured it around his neck. She then pulled out a penlight, checking his pupil response for any signs of neurological damage.

As they worked, the heat from the nearby car fire intensified. The wind carried waves of scorching air toward them, making the urgency of their task even more pressing. Just as Maggie finished securing the collar, the fire department arrived. A powerful stream of water and foam doused the flames, hissing against the wreckage.

With practiced efficiency, Maggie and Nicole completed Bill's stabilization, securing him onto a backboard before transferring him to the stretcher. Nearby, another team of paramedics continued working on the driver of the second vehicle. With Bill safely loaded into the ambulance, they departed for University Hospital.

Upon arrival, they wheeled Bill through the emergency room doors. As they handed him off to the hospital staff, the second ambulance team rushed in with another patient from the crash. The man on the stretcher wore a tuxedo shirt, bow tie, and black pants. A breathing tube had been placed in his trachea, and one of the paramedics rhythmically squeezed a resuscitation bag to keep him breathing. A large white gauze pad, already stained with blood, covered the side of his face.

Maggie and Nicole paused, watching as the team hurried past them. The gravity of the situation settled over them. Just then, Matt, a police officer from the crash scene, entered the ER and made his way toward Nicole.

Hey, Matt, were you at the scene?" Nicole extended her hand.

Yeah." Matt shook it firmly. This guy had open booze bottles in his car. He was a mess. No seatbelt, so he went headfirst into the windshield. Your patient was just sitting at a red light when this guy slammed into another car from behind."

Damn. Our guy should be okay—bumps, burns, nothing too serious. He was lucky to make it out of that car."

You got that right." Matt sighed, rubbing the back of his neck. Hey, we re throwing a birthday party for Rebecca at Buddy s pool hall after our shift. You two in? She d love to see you both."

Rebecca and Matt had been married a year.

I ll be there. Maggie probably needs to get home," Nicole started.

Actually, count me in." Maggie interrupted.

Nicole turned, raising an eyebrow. Really?"

Matt grinned. Great. See you both there. I gotta run—paperwork s calling." He gave them a quick wave before heading off.

Back at the ambulance, Maggie and Nicole climbed into the back of the unit and started cleaning up.

Nicole shot Maggie a sideways glance. Okay, what was that about?"

Maggie smirked. What?"

You never go out after work."

Maggie hesitated, her hands busy wiping down the stretcher. I know. I just don t want to go home right away tonight."

Nicole s playful expression softened. Everything okay?"

Maggie let out a small breath. Nothing I haven t dealt with before." A pause. I don t really want to talk about it." Then, shifting the conversation, Hey, did you ever find out about Gary?"

Nicole exhaled sharply. Yeah. Found him the next day. He said he never saw her again after leaving my house."

Maggie studied her. "That's it?"

Nicole tossed a used gauze wrapper into the trash. "Yeah. I told him to stay away. I'm done." She stopped cleaning, leaning back against the wall of the ambulance.

Maggie reached for her hand, giving it a squeeze. "Are you gonna be okay? You've spent your whole life looking out for him."

"It has to stop. I can't trust him." Nicole stared at the floor, falling silent for a few moments.

Maggie gave her a reassuring pat on the knee. "Come on, let's clean up and finish our paperwork. I'm really looking forward to a margarita tonight." She stood and resumed wiping down the unit.

They finished the rest of their shift without much conversation, then drove separately to Buddy's Pool Hall.

Nicole arrived first, stepping outside to wait for Maggie. When she spotted her approaching, she pulled open the heavy front door, letting her step inside first. The place was dimly lit, the air thick with a stale carpet smell. A row of pool tables stretched along one side, while dart machines hummed quietly in the background. On the opposite side, a small dance floor sat mostly empty, surrounded by high-top tables.

Toward the back of the room, Matt stood from one of the tables, raising a hand to get their attention.

Nicole nudged Maggie. "Why don't you go say hello to Rebecca? I'll get the drinks. Margarita for you, right?"

Maggie smiled. "Double. Thanks. I'll get the next round."

She made her way toward the long table where about ten people sat, most of them either in police uniforms or hospital scrubs. Rebecca, once a nurse at University Hospital's ER, had traded in her scrubs for a badge after earning her degree in Criminal Justice. The pay cut had been worth it—she was finally doing something that made her happy.

Seeing Maggie approach, Rebecca stood, her face lighting up. "I'm so glad you made it!" She pulled Maggie into a warm hug, wrapping both arms around her neck.

"Me too. Happy birthday! You look amazing." Maggie squeezed her tightly before pulling back.

Nicole arrived just in time, handing Maggie her drink before shifting to Rebecca. Balancing her beer in one hand, she wrapped the other arm around Rebecca in a quick hug.

"Look at you, the birthday girl." Nicole grinned, pressing a quick kiss to Rebecca's cheek.

After the greetings were over, they settled into their seats, conversations flowing easily around the table. Maggie let out a slow breath, allowing herself to relax. It felt good to be out, surrounded by friends—something she rarely did anymore.

Still, an unwelcome thought crept into her mind. Victor. She recalled how cruel he had been the other night, the sting of his words still fresh. Shaking it off, she signaled for another drink.

As the night wore on, Maggie drank more heavily. Within an hour, she had downed three margaritas, the warmth of the alcohol dulling the weight she had been carrying. The table slowly emptied as people said their goodbyes, until only Matt, Rebecca, Nicole, and Maggie remained.

Rebecca grinned, leaning into Matt. "One more round."

Matt shook his head, wrapping an arm around her. "Oh no, you don't, birthday girl. You've had enough."

Come on, one more! You party pooper," Maggie slurred, laughing as she leaned into Nicole.

Matt's voice turned firm. "No, no, no. You two have had way too much to drink, and neither of you is driving home."

Maggie waved a hand dismissively. "I'm fine." The room wobbled slightly, her head feeling far too heavy for her neck. She turned to Nicole, blinking.

Nicole sighed. "I'll drive you home. You can pick up your car tomorrow. I'll come get you for work, and we'll swing by here to grab it."

Maggie opened her mouth to respond, then forgot what she was about to say. She frowned, her face momentarily blank.

Matt and Nicole burst out laughing. "Okay," Maggie giggled, shrugging.

Matt and Nicole helped the two women up, steadying them as they made their way to the front door. Nicole tightened her grip around Maggie's waist, keeping her upright.

"Easy now. And no getting sick in my car!" she teased.

"Promise," Maggie giggled.

Nicole secured Maggie into the passenger seat and waved goodnight to Matt and Rebecca before climbing behind the wheel. She glanced at Maggie, who had slumped against the center armrest, resting her head in her hand.

"You gonna be all right?" Nicole asked, her voice softer now.

Maggie didn't answer right away. Her gaze was blank, unfocused, as she stared at Nicole, lost somewhere deep inside her own thoughts.

You re really nice. I don t know if I ever told you, but I really think you re a nice girl." Maggie emphasized the word *really*, her eyes heavy-lidded as she smiled up at Nicole.

Nicole smirked. Okay. I m *really* nice. Now, let s get you home before Victor starts worrying." She mimicked Maggie s tone playfully.

Maggie leaned back against the seat, running a hand through her hair. Screw him. I don t care if Victor s mad. He doesn t care about me." Her voice softened as she turned to stare out the passenger window.

Nicole frowned. Sure, he does. What s going on?"

She hadn t started the engine yet. Instead, she studied Maggie, who seemed lost in a drunken haze. Before Nicole could say anything else, Maggie lifted a finger to her lips, pressing it gently against them.

Shhh. I don t want to think about it."

Her head swayed slightly, her finger still resting against Nicole s mouth. Then, her eyes fluttered closed, her body sinking deeper into the seat as if she might pass out.

Nicole s heart pounded. A strange, fluttering warmth bloomed in her stomach. Without thinking, she closed her eyes and pressed a soft kiss to the tip of Maggie s finger.

Maggie pulled her hand back, resting it on her lap, her eyes still closed.

Nicole swallowed hard, inhaling sharply before finally turning the key in the ignition. Her thoughts raced, her pulse unsteady. The desire she had buried for so long surged through her, but she knew Maggie was too far gone, lost in the alcohol.

The drive was silent. Maggie kept her eyes closed, whether in thought or sleep, Nicole couldn t tell.

When they pulled into the driveway, Nicole reached over and gently touched Maggie's arm. "We're here."

Maggie stirred, stretching slightly before covering her face with her hands. She hesitated before lowering them.

"Do you want me to help you inside?" Nicole asked softly.

Maggie blinked, then shook her head. "No, I can make it. Thanks for the ride."

She stepped out, wobbling slightly before catching herself. Turning back, she smiled.

"I'll pick you up at two o'clock," Nicole reminded her.

"Be careful." Maggie rummaged through her purse, searching for her keys.

Nicole didn't leave until she saw Maggie safely inside.

As she drove home, she couldn't shake the feeling of Maggie's soft finger against her lips. She wanted to tell her—wanted to *admit* what she had felt for so long. But the fear of losing what little they already had kept her silent.

Instead, she let the moment drift away, just as she always had.

And when she got home, she crawled into bed, staring at the ceiling, trying not to think about what it would feel like to *really* kiss her.

CHAPTER NINE

Maggie stretched beneath the floral-patterned comforter, arms reaching as a deep yawn escaped her lips. She squinted against the intrusive daylight, shielding her eyes with one hand. Parting two fingers slightly, she managed to peek through one barely opened eye, catching a blurry glimpse of the alarm clock beside her bed.

One o clock in the afternoon.

With a sigh, she let her fingers close again, as if shutting out the time would somehow make it go away. The thought of dragging herself out of bed and into work felt unbearable. Her head pounded—a dull, relentless reminder of the margaritas she d downed last night.

Slowly, she forced her hand away from her face, blinking against the brightness as she struggled to piece together the evening s events. Drinking—definitely too much. Nicole—driving her home. *Thank God for Nicole.* Then—what else?

A glimpse of white caught her eye. On the pillow next to hers, a small note rested where Victor had slept. Maggie reached for it, turning it over in her fingers.

"I love you."

She exhaled through her nose, rolling her eyes as she read his name at the bottom. *Great.* She wasn't in the mood for sentimentality this morning—*or afternoon*, technically. Groaning, she tossed the note onto the nightstand and trudged toward the bathroom, Wrangler following at her heels.

"I don't have time for a walk today, boy," she muttered, glancing down as his ears perked. He flopped onto the floor near the door, watching her with disappointed eyes.

Twenty minutes later, Maggie emerged from the shower, dressed and feeling marginally more human. She threw together a sandwich for lunch, refilled Wrangler's food and water bowls, and had just taken a long sip of coffee when the sound of a car horn cut through the quiet.

She didn't need to look outside to know it was Nicole.

Sliding on a pair of dark sunglasses—her last defense against the merciless daylight—Maggie grabbed her bag and stepped outside.

Nicole smirked as Maggie climbed into the passenger seat. "Good morning."

Maggie groaned. "Don't even start with me. How could you let me get so drunk? I *totally* hold you responsible."

Nicole chuckled as she pulled away from the curb, her eyes dancing with amusement. "Oh, please. Like I could stop you."

The bar where they'd met last night wasn't far, and soon, they arrived at the station house. Maggie grabbed a large cup of coffee from the break room while Nicole retrieved their unit keys.

Even with the caffeine in hand, Maggie refused to remove her sunglasses. The light was still too cruel.

The dispatch came in suddenly, urgent, and clear.

"Unit 4-7, report to North Star Mall. Drive-by shooting, one juvenile male victim, GSW to the chest. Shooter still at large. Exercise extreme caution."

Nicole flipped the switch, activating the siren and flashing lights as she pressed down on the gas. The patrol car surged forward, weaving through traffic with precision. Maggie gripped the dashboard, her body tensing.

"A kid. Damn it."

When they arrived, the scene was chaos. Police vehicles blocked off sections of the parking lot, their lights strobing against the concrete. A small crowd had gathered, their murmurs blending into a dull roar. Officers worked to control the bystanders, some pushing them back, others scanning the area for any sign of the shooter.

Near the center of it all, an officer knelt over the injured boy, pressing a blood-soaked towel to his chest. The pavement beneath him glistened with fresh crimson. The officer turned, his gloved hand smeared red as he waved them over.

Hurry up! He's bleeding out!" he yelled.

Maggie and Nicole rushed forward. The victim was young—maybe fifteen—his face pale, his breaths shallow. A red bandana wrapped around his head, and his exposed arms and shoulders were covered in tattoos. His torn white tank top was stained with blood, ripped open to reveal the gaping wound in his chest.

Maggie dropped to her knees, yanking sterile gauze from her bag and pressing it firmly against the wound. "We need to control the bleeding!" she said, her voice steady but urgent.

Nicole leaned in, checking for a pulse. "No pulse. Not breathing," she announced, already shifting into action. She grabbed an airway tube from their kit, signaling a nearby officer. "Start chest compressions!"

The officer immediately positioned himself and began the rhythmic compressions, his hands pressing down with controlled force. Nicole worked swiftly, inserting the airway tube into the boy's trachea.

Maggie frowned as blood continued to seep through the gauze. "We're losing too much blood. Let's roll him—see if there's an exit wound."

Nicole nodded and moved to help, but before they could turn him, a deafening BANG rang out—sharp, echoing through the parking garage like a thunderclap.

"Shots fired."

Get down!" a police officer roared.

Nicole reacted instantly, grabbing Maggie and pulling her to the ground. Maggie barely had time to register what was happening before she found herself pinned beneath Nicole, their faces just inches apart.

Maggie's breath hitched. She could see the fear flicker in Nicole's eyes, her adrenaline-fueled heartbeat pounding against her chest.

"Maggie, are you okay?" Nicole's voice was urgent, her breath warm against Maggie's cheek.

Maggie swallowed hard, trying to push away the shock and the proximity of their closeness.

"I'm fine," she whispered.

It's okay! Just a car backfiring. All clear!"

The voice echoed through the parking garage, cutting through the tension like a blade.

Nicole exhaled sharply, her grip loosening as she peeled herself off Maggie. Their moment of fear, the heart-pounding intensity, dissolved into a lingering unease. No gunshots. No shooter. But the boy beneath them was still bleeding out.

Nicole immediately refocused, her hands moving with practiced urgency as she inserted an artificial airway into the boy's trachea. Maggie, steadying her own nerves, swiftly slid an intravenous catheter into his arm. The two of them worked in sync, their movements precise and instinctual.

"Let's move!"

They lifted the boy onto the stretcher, Maggie climbing into the back of the ambulance while Nicole jumped into the driver's seat. A police officer from the scene joined Maggie, taking over the airway as she resumed chest compressions. The ambulance jolted forward, sirens wailing as they sped toward University Hospital.

Maggie pressed down again and again, her hands locked together over the boy's chest, willing his heart to beat. But deep down, she already knew. It was too late.

His skin was cold beneath her touch. His face, once full of youth, was pale and lifeless. Blood still smeared his torn tank top, a stark contrast to the innocence he should have still possessed.

He's just a kid.

But she kept going, her arms aching with each compression. She had to. Even if her body screamed for rest. Even if she knew it was useless.

She had to try.

The ambulance skidded to a stop outside the ER doors, the back doors flying open as medical staff rushed to take over. The ER team worked frantically—pumping fluids, shocking his heart, trying desperately to replace what had already been lost on the pavement.

Maggie stood in the corner, watching. Waiting. Praying.

But at 9:30 p.m., the doctor's voice cut through the room with finality.

"Time of death, 9:30 p.m."

The words echoed, and suddenly, the hospital felt too bright. Too sterile. Too empty.

Maggie swallowed hard. Her hands, still stained with his blood, felt numb.

The ride back to the station was silent. Nicole drove, her grip tight on the wheel. Maggie sat in the passenger seat, staring out into the night, the city lights blurring into a haze.

Between them, the weight of what had just happened lingered—thick, suffocating.

Back at the station, they moved methodically, wiping the blood from the ambulance floor, scrubbing away the only traces left of a life lost too soon. The scent of antiseptic filled the air, but it couldn't erase the memory. The boy's face. His stillness. The feeling of his body growing colder beneath her hands.

Maggie felt the lump in her throat rise again. She swallowed it down. They weren't supposed to get emotional. Not on the job. Not where people counted on them to be strong.

She showered at the station house before heading home. Blood had soaked through her uniform pants while she performed CPR on the young boy—another call she wouldn't be able to forget. After changing, she made the short drive back, her body heavy with exhaustion.

She couldn't tell if the fatigue came from the emotional toll of the last dispatch or the lingering hangover from the night before. Either way, a faint sense of relief washed over her as she pulled her BMW into the garage.

The house was quiet as she stepped through the back door. A soft glow came from the family room. Victor was still up, sitting in his usual chair with a book open in his lap.

Wrangler wagged his tail and trotted over, tail swishing eagerly against the floor.

Hey, what are you doing up so late?" Maggie asked, crouching to scratch behind Wrangler's ears.

Victor stood and crossed the room, closing the book as he came toward her. *I wanted to be awake when you got home."*

He wrapped his arms gently around her waist, and she leaned into him, grateful for the solidness of his presence.

"I'm very sorry about the other night. Can you forgive me?"

Maggie hesitated. Her muscles tensed under his touch, remembering the way his words had cut into her the last time they spoke. His anger, the sharp tone, the frustration he had taken out on her.

"I don't like when you treat me that way."

She turned her head away slightly, resisting the tenderness in his kisses.

Victor sighed, stepping back just enough to meet her eyes. "I had a really bad day at work. The market dropped, and I made a bad investment. I shouldn't have taken it out on you."

An excuse. Maggie wasn't sure if she fully bought it, but she said nothing.

He must have sensed her hesitation because he smiled and lifted two pieces of paper from the side table.

"I'm not coming to you empty-handed and begging for forgiveness. I plan on making it up to you."

Maggie narrowed her eyes, curiosity flickering through the exhaustion. "Oh yeah? What do you mean?"

Victor's smirk grew. "I have two tickets and hotel reservations for the Cayman Islands. We leave on Friday."

Maggie blinked. "You're crazy. I can't go on vacation."

"Yes, you can." He took a step closer, his voice smooth, confident. "I already spoke to Mike. Starting Friday, you have one glorious week off from work."

She frowned. "Wait... *Mike* approved this?"

Victor nodded, looking proud of himself. "He said you needed a break. And so do I. What do you think? It will be great."

Maggie studied Victor's face, searching for any sign that he might be joking. But he wasn't. His excitement was genuine.

A slow smile tugged at her lips before she reached up and kissed him.

"You're amazing," she murmured against his lips. "My gosh, the Cayman Islands... where exactly is that?"

Victor chuckled, gently pulling her toward the couch. "Come sit down. I have some brochures and printed information from the internet." He wrapped his arms around her waist, pulling her close. "Are you happy?"

Maggie hesitated for just a fraction of a second before nodding. "Yes, I m happy."

But a thought lingered at the back of her mind. She pulled back slightly, studying him again. "Can we afford this?"

Victor s expression didn t change. "Don t worry, everything is taken care of." His voice was smooth, reassuring.

Maggie wanted to believe him, but doubt flickered inside her. She had learned to recognize the difference between Victor s confidence and his deflections, and she wasn t sure which this was.

"Except for Wrangler," Victor continued. "Do you think Nicole could watch him for a week? I d hate to put him in a kennel."

Maggie glanced at the dog curled up on the floor, his ears twitching as if he knew he was being talked about. She smiled, feeling a pang of guilt. "I bet she would. I ll ask her tomorrow."

Still holding Victor s hand, she let him lead her to the couch. They sat together, flipping through glossy brochures filled with pictures of turquoise waters, white sand beaches, and luxurious resorts.

CHAPTER TEN

Good morning," Maggie said with a broad smile as she walked to the rear of the ambulance. The sun shone bright, with no clouds to obscure the vast blue sky.

Nicole leaned against the back of the ambulance, her head tilted back, eyes closed, and face turned toward the sun. Her shirtsleeves were rolled up halfway, exposing her arms to the heat. The weather was hot and dry, with the forecast predicting a high of 95 degrees for the San Antonio area. Slowly, she brought her head forward and looked at Maggie.

My, someone s in a chipper mood today," Nicole said with a smile.

Yes, I am," Maggie replied, slipping her hands into the pockets of her tactical 5.11 cargo pants.

Guess where I m going tomorrow?" she teased, acting as if she held a big secret.

Hmmm... let me see. Could it be the Cayman Islands?" Nicole remained leaning against the ambulance, arms crossed over her chest.

You re a brat! Who told you?" Maggie playfully narrowed her eyes.

Mike told me earlier today. And guess who I get to ride with while you re gone?" Nicole said with a keen expression.

Who?" Maggie asked curiously.

Jamie Preston. Thank you very much!" Nicole teased.

Jamie... oh my, he s going to talk your ear off," Maggie said with a grin, playfully punching Nicole s arm.

Don t remind me."

Hey, just think how much you ll appreciate me when I get back." Maggie walked around to the passenger side of the ambulance and climbed into the seat.

Nicole didn t respond. Instead, she opened the driver s door and stepped into the vehicle.

What s the plan?" she asked, hesitating as she glanced at Maggie.

Let s go wash the unit. Then can we stop by a department store? I need to pick up some suntan lotion. If I don t go now, I know I ll forget. Hey, by the way, can you stay at my place and dog-sit while we re away? I know it s a last-minute request." Maggie s tone shifted to a pleading one.

Sure, not a problem," Nicole said as she drove away from the station house.

The rest of their shift went smoothly, with only a few dispatches. They spent the remainder of the evening at the station house. Maggie sat working on her peer reviews while Nicole played cards with the dispatch operator. From where Nicole sat, she could see Maggie through the doorway. She stole occasional glances, watching as Maggie stretched and ran a hand through her hair. Occasionally, Maggie would look up, almost catching Nicole staring at her. Each time, Nicole quickly looked away and struck up a conversation with the dispatch operator.

About an hour before the end of their shift, a call came through dispatch requesting an ambulance. A homeless man had found a woman in an alleyway downtown, her body severely beaten and raped. At that point, there was no word on whether she was dead or alive.

Maggie and Nicole volunteered to take the call. However, Ben assigned the dispatch to another unit closer to the area. Maggie s first thought was of Detective Mallory. Her second thought was of Gary. She wished Nicole had never confided in her about finding Gary beating the prostitute the night before she was murdered. Maggie had already harbored uneasy feelings about him, and these new details only heightened her suspicions. She recalled what Nicole had mentioned about Gary showing up at her apartment with cut hands and other troubling incidents she had shared.

Maggie s heart began to race. She glanced at Nicole, debating whether to bring up her concerns. In the end, she decided against it. She didn t want to add to Nicole s distress, knowing how conflicted she already felt about the situation. Besides, it would be wrong to make accusations without solid proof. Taking a deep breath, Maggie forced herself to stop thinking about Gary.

When her shift ended, Maggie left work and drove the short distance home. Excitement bubbled inside her at the thought of their upcoming trip to the Cayman Islands. She hadn t traveled much in her life, and the few places she had visited were mostly within the United States. She wondered if the breathtaking images in travel magazines were real or if photographers had some secret technique for making the waters appear so vivid and clear.

She tried to imagine a place where the ocean shimmered as blue as the sky and the beaches stretched out in pure white sand. A smile crossed her lips as she pulled her car into the garage, parking next to her husband s.

Maggie entered the house and immediately heard the sound of running water from the upstairs shower. Wrangler greeted her at the door, his tail wagging, and she gave his head a quick pat before making her way up the stairs. The bathroom door was slightly open, and a misty steam filled the small room.

She quickly undressed in the hallway, leaving her clothes on the floor, then quietly pushed the bathroom door open and slipped inside. Through the shower curtain, she could see Victor s silhouette as he washed his hair. Smirking, she pulled back the curtain and slid her body into the small shower.

Boo," she whispered, reaching over to kiss him as he wiped the water from his eyes.

Hey, you re home," he said, pulling her closer. Are you excited?"

More than you know," she teased, sliding her hands up his thigh toward his groin.

My wife s frisky tonight, huh?" he chuckled. You ll need a cold shower because we need sleep—we have an early flight." He stepped out of the shower and turned the temperature knob to cold.

Maggie let out a playful scream, quickly reaching for the knob to turn the water back to hot. You wait—paybacks are a bitch," she laughed, closing the curtain after he stepped out.

Did you talk to Nicole about watching Wrangler?" Victor asked as he moved to the sink and began brushing his teeth.

Yes, she s going to do it. I gave her my extra key. She ll come over in the morning after we leave." Maggie finished her shower, dried off, and wrapped herself in a towel. Did you stop by the grocery store on the way home?"

Crap—I knew I forgot something."

It s okay. I ll just leave her some money on the counter so she can pick up some milk, bread, or whatever she needs. She probably won t eat here anyway." As she walked past him, she playfully tugged the towel from around his waist, letting it fall to the floor.

Hey!" he yelled, standing there naked with a toothbrush in his mouth. Maggie giggled as she hurried past him.

They climbed into bed, and Maggie snuggled beneath the comforter, letting out a contented sigh.

Are you sure you don t feel like starting our vacation early?" she murmured seductively, sliding her hand into his boxers.

Victor chuckled and gently removed her hand. Go to sleep," he said, smiling as he reached for the nightstand and switched off the light.

Maggie let out another loud sigh in the darkness.

CHAPTER ELEVEN

Maggie woke early and eagerly slipped out of bed, pulling open the curtains that covered the large sliding glass doors leading onto the balcony. It was only seven o clock in the morning, but the sun was already shining brightly. She opened the door and stepped outside, the warm air wrapping around her as a strong, humid breeze rolled in from the ocean.

Squinting against the brilliant sunlight, she lifted a hand to shield her eyes. As she gazed out over the vast expanse of water, she inhaled deeply, filling her lungs with the fresh, salty air. A smile spread across her lips.

Their oceanfront room was on the fifth floor of the Bombay Resort, located along Seven Mile Beach—a prime area for visitors to Grand Cayman Island. The sweeping white sand, kissed by the lapping azure waves, created a breathtakingly serene landscape.

Standing there, mesmerized by the stunning surroundings, Maggie felt certain that if paradise truly existed, it had to be here. The vibrant ocean colors matched the images she had admired in travel magazines, and the water s clarity extended nearly a hundred feet down, revealing a kaleidoscope of colorful fish and coral formations swaying beneath the surface.

Victor stirred awake and soon joined her on the balcony. Sleepy-eyed and barefoot, he walked up behind her, wrapping his arms around her body and resting his chin on her shoulder. Clad only in silk boxers, he let out a long yawn.

How do you like it?" he murmured.

I never want to leave," she breathed. This is amazing. Thank you for making this happen—for me and for us."

Victor kissed her shoulder. What would you like to do today?"

Well, for starters, let s get dressed and have some breakfast. Then we can pick up a rental car and do some shopping. I m so excited!"

Maggie turned, clenched her fists in front of her, and tightened her body with anticipation. Then, unable to contain her enthusiasm, she eagerly walked back into their elegantly decorated room. Victor laughed, watching her prance around as she excitedly got ready.

During breakfast, Maggie sifted through several brochures she had picked up at the front desk. The resort offered a buffet-style breakfast with a mix of American favorites and local Caribbean dishes. Unable to resist, Maggie filled her plate to the brim with eggs, sausage, potatoes, fresh fruit, and pastries.

She and Victor chose a table outside beneath a large coconut tree beside the swimming pool. The morning sun cast a golden glow over the water, and a gentle breeze rustled the palm fronds above them.

Gee, what an appetite you have today," Victor teased, eyeing Maggie s overflowing plate with an amused smile.

I m starving! I want to try everything." She grinned before handing him a few of the brochures she had already looked through. Take a look at these."

Victor flipped through them casually before holding up one. What about this?" He pointed to a pamphlet advertising scuba diving lessons.

Maggie hesitated, her expression shifting from curiosity to surprise. You're joking, right?" she asked, staring at Victor.

No, I think it would be great," he said, unfazed. You've never tried it before. It's an incredible experience—seeing everything up close, being sixty feet underwater while fish swim all around you. It's like entering another world. Come on, don't you want to try?" He smiled as he continued eating.

Maggie studied him for a moment, her fork hovering over her plate.

Victor... isn't that how your first wife died? Scuba diving?" Her voice carried a note of hesitation.

Victor exhaled deeply, closing his eyes for a second before rubbing his temple with one hand. His lips pressed into a thin line.

Yes," he admitted quietly. Linda died while scuba diving in Honduras. But it was an accident. It's a very safe activity, I promise. I would never let anything happen to you." His eyes softened as he looked at Maggie, eyebrows lifting in an apologetic expression.

You don't have to apologize to me," Maggie said gently. I just... I was thinking about how you'd feel doing it again. I thought you once told me it happened here, in the Cayman Islands." She frowned slightly, confused. Have you been diving since then?"

Yes. I had to get back in the water," Victor said, setting down his fork. I didn't want fear controlling my life." He glanced at Maggie, his expression unreadable. And it was Honduras, not the Caymans. But we don t have to do it if you re not comfortable." He resumed eating, seemingly indifferent to the conversation.

Maggie reached across the table, placing her hand over his.

If you want to go, I ll try it," she said softly. But I have to admit—it s going to be scary." She leaned over and kissed his cheek.

Victor s lips curved into a small smile. Great. I ll set it up for later." His eyes brightened. Oh, and there s this place called Stingray City I want to take you to. We can snorkel with the stingrays. The water s only about fifteen feet deep, and it s in the middle of the ocean. It s supposed to be amazing."

Sounds great," Maggie said, though her smile wavered. Stingrays... aren t they poisonous?" She raised an eyebrow in mock suspicion.

Victor chuckled. No, don t worry. It ll be fine."

After breakfast, Victor stopped by the concierge desk and rented a Jeep for the remainder of their stay. He also booked a Discover Scuba lesson for Maggie—a beginner s program designed to give non-divers a taste of the underwater world without the full certification course. For dive shops, it was an easy way to introduce tourists to the sport while making a tidy profit.

Since Victor was already a certified diver, he would accompany Maggie on the dive. However, a trained instructor would stay by her side throughout the entire underwater excursion.

The Cayman Islands were world-famous for their diving diversity, attracting enthusiasts from across the globe. Nestled in the Caribbean Sea, the archipelago consisted of three small islands, located roughly 480 miles south of Miami—just a short one-hour flight from the U.S. Known for its safety, crystal-clear waters, and laid-back charm, the Cayman Islands offered the perfect balance of British sophistication and Caribbean hospitality. With an average year-round temperature of 80°F, pristine beaches, and duty-free shopping, it was a dream destination for vacationers.

Maggie and Victor packed a day bag with a few island essentials—sunscreen, tissues, extra towels, and bottled water—before heading outside to find their rental Jeep parked in front of the hotel.

They spent the afternoon exploring the island, taking in its lush landscapes, charming seaside towns, and breathtaking ocean views. By early evening, they returned to their resort just in time for dinner—a lavish buffet served beside the swimming pool, illuminated by the soft glow of tiki torches.

Stuffed from their meal, they took a leisurely stroll along the beach, the sand cool beneath their feet. The sunset painted the sky with brilliant streaks of blue, orange, red, and gold, its reflection shimmering across the gentle waves.

"This is amazing," Maggie sighed, resting her head against Victor's shoulder.

"Hmmm, yes, it is," he murmured, squeezing her hand.

She exhaled contentedly. "We should probably get back and get some sleep since you have us scheduled for an underwater adventure tomorrow." She gave him a playful glance.

Victor slid an arm around her waist, pulling her close. "Yeah, you're right. You'll see—it's going to be incredible."

Maggie smirked, nudging him. "Hmm, let's go to bed'... now that sounds like a pretty good idea."

Laughing, they walked hand in hand back toward the hotel, the ocean breeze wrapping around them like a warm embrace.

CHAPTER TWELVE

Maggie stood at the edge near the back of the boat, her hair pulled back into a ponytail, a diving mask tightly secured to her face, and a breathing regulator clenched between her teeth. She wore rental diving gear: a buoyancy control device (BCD), a weight belt around her waist, and large pink fins on her feet. Nervous yet excited, she waited for her instructor to clear her for entry into the water. Her heart raced, beating faster with anticipation. She focused on breathing slowly through the regulator, just as she d been taught during the scuba lesson.

Victor sat on a nearby bench, already in his diving gear, smiling as he watched her.

"One, two, three... go," said the young, well-built, tanned instructor as he gave Maggie a slight nudge, helping her make her entry into the water. He followed right behind her, also in full diving gear.

With her eyes wide open, Maggie looked around in every direction as her body slowly descended into the blue abyss. The sound of her own breathing through the regulator was all she could hear. Her instructor faced her, holding her arms, coaching her to keep clearing her ears as they sank deeper. At about sixty feet, he signaled for her to level off and assisted her in adding just enough air to her BCD to stop her descent. Her body hovered steady and buoyant.

Maggie concentrated on her breathing and gazed in awe at the colorful fish surrounding her. Aside from her breathing, she could hear faint crackling sounds, shrimp crawling along the sandy ocean bottom. In the distance, she spotted Victor waving at her. She smiled, and a little water leaked into the corner of her mask. Victor blew her a kiss before following the two other divers who were assigned as his partners.

Allowing herself to float with the Yellow Snappers, Parrot Fish, Tangs, and Clown Fish, Maggie let her body go limp. The underwater world was alive, bursting with life and color, from the darting fish to the vibrant corals.

Thirty minutes passed in what felt like an instant. Maggie began her slow ascent. When she reached the surface, her body bobbed with the rhythm of the waves. She swam back to the ladder dangling from the side of the boat.

"Wow! Now that was wonderful," she exclaimed, removing the regulator from her mouth. She climbed the ladder and peeled off her dive gear. Victor handed her a towel.

"See? I told you," he said, drying his hair with his own towel. He grabbed a couple of bottled waters from a cooler on deck and motioned for Maggie to follow.

Let s sit on the bow of the boat for the ride back. Maybe we ll get lucky and see some dolphins."

Maggie joined him at the front of the boat. They admired the ocean s beauty, sharing stories about what they d seen during the dive. The thirty-minute ride back to the dock passed peacefully.

After a short nap under a palm tree on the beach, Maggie and Victor returned to their room to shower and get ready for dinner. It was Friday night, and the resort was hosting local bands for outdoor dining.

Maggie and Victor had reserved a table by the pool with a perfect view of the ocean.

A cool breeze rustled the palm trees, their shadows dancing under the moonlight. The moon cast a shimmering glow across the ocean's surface. The sound of distant waves breaking on the shore blended with the island music drifting through the air.

What can I get you to drink?" asked a young, dark-skinned server with striking light green eyes. She wore a floral-patterned blouse and black pants. A thick silver choker adorned her neck, its unique design catching Maggie's eye.

Yes, two margaritas with no salt, please," Victor replied.

I love your necklace. Did you buy it here on the island?" Maggie asked.

No, I bought this last year in St. Thomas. A local artist made it. It's one of a kind," the girl said, touching her necklace as she glanced at Victor, then back at Maggie.

It's so beautiful," Maggie said. The server smiled again, blushing as she turned to get their drinks. Maggie laughed, nudging Victor.

I think she's flirting with you. Did you see the way she smiled at you?" she teased.

No, no, no," Victor replied modestly, his face slightly flushed.

The server soon returned with their drinks. Before leaving, Victor ordered another. He removed the umbrella and straw and sipped his margarita until the glass was half-empty.

Slow down—we have all night. You're probably dehydrated from the sun. Want some water?" Maggie asked.

Victor didn't respond. He stared at the dance floor, distracted. Maggie looked in the same direction and repeated her question, this time a little louder. Still, no response.

"Hello?" she said, nearly yelling, waving her hand in front of his face. "Are we here together?"

"What?" he answered sarcastically.

"I'm sorry—did I interrupt something? I was talking to you."

Victor gulped the rest of his drink, tossed the straw from the second margarita onto the table, and drank that one down quickly, too. He waved to the server for another.

Maggie watched, exasperated. She shook her head and turned away.

"Can you just back off and stop asking so many questions?" Victor said coldly as he stood up, drink in hand. "You know what—never mind. I'm going for a walk. I'm not hungry. I'll see you back in the room."

Before she could respond, he walked off. On the way, he snatched the next margarita from the server's tray, smiling and exchanging a few words with her before disappearing toward the beach.

Maggie felt her face flush with anger, her body trembling. She held out her hand to confirm what she already knew—she was shaking. She brushed her hair back and folded her arms, taking a deep breath. Tears welled up as she paced her breaths, trying not to cry.

She ordered room service, settled the tab for Victor's drinks, and headed back to the hotel room. As she walked through the darkness, the tears she'd been holding back began to fall freely.

This week on the island had been everything she thought they needed. She felt close to him again. Happy. Relaxed. Time together had always been the missing piece. But now, the week was tainted once more by his cold indifference. Something she couldn't control.

Back in the room, she took a hot shower, packed her suitcase, and crawled into bed. They were leaving the next afternoon. She hoped against what she knew—that Victor would come in and apologize. She drifted to sleep, still hoping.

Maggie rolled over and reached across the bed, finding only an empty space. She kept her eyes closed and took a deep breath, exhaling like it was a chore. Morning sunlight pushed through the curtains, warming her skin. She covered her eyes with one hand, shielding herself from the day.

Finally, the door opened. Maggie opened her eyes and saw Victor, still in the same clothes from last night.

"Are you just coming in?" she asked, her voice tight with anger.

"I slept in a hammock by the pool. I swear, I think I've been eaten alive." He scratched his arms and neck.

"I'm going to take a shower. We need to get moving. I don't want to miss the flight. I have a taxi arranged for pickup in an hour," he said, closing the bathroom door behind him.

Maggie stayed in bed, her hand still over her eyes. She felt the wetness of tears in her palm. With a frustrated sigh, she threw off the covers and pounded the bed with her fist.

She forced herself to get moving, choosing her clothes for the trip home.

They checked out at the front desk and waited outside for the taxi. A small, beat-up yellow car with "TAXI" painted on the door pulled up.

Hello," the dark-skinned elderly driver greeted them in a warm island accent. He helped Victor load the suitcases into the trunk.

Our flight leaves in an hour and a half. We need to get to the airport pronto," Victor said.

No problem, man. You have plenty of time," the driver replied.

Victor sat up front, while Maggie sat in back, staring silently out the window. Her emotions were tangled—sadness, anger, and confusion rolled into one.

Trying to lighten the mood, the driver glanced in the rearview mirror. So, did you enjoy your stay on our beautiful island?"

After a few seconds of silence, Maggie realized Victor wouldn t answer.

Yes," she replied politely. It s a beautiful island. Have you always lived here?"

Yes, ma am. My family s been here for generations—my grandfather and his grandfather before him," he chuckled.

Ah..." the driver muttered, and the car began to slow.

What s wrong?" Maggie asked, noticing they were stuck behind a line of vehicles.

The police have something blocked up ahead. Maybe an accident. These crazy foreign drivers," he joked, glancing at Victor.

Victor stayed quiet.

The driver pulled onto the shoulder and maneuvered around the other cars, ignoring their honking as he pushed forward.

Come on, come on," he muttered as they passed the scene—police, a local ambulance, and a group of bystanders.

Maggie looked out the side window, then back through the rear window. She saw no damaged vehicles but noticed an ambulance crew comforting an older woman who was crying. A black body bag on a stretcher confirmed something tragic had happened.

The rest of the ride to the airport took only twenty minutes. The small terminal resembled a heavily guarded warehouse more than an international airport.

See? No problem," the driver said as he opened the trunk and handed Victor their luggage.

Victor gave him a ten-dollar tip.

They had just enough time to pass through customs and check in for their flight. Neither spoke. Maggie read a book while Victor napped during the entire flight.

The drive home was uneventful and silent.

Relief washed over Maggie when she stepped into her home. Nothing felt better than returning.

CHAPTER THIRTEEN

Hey, welcome back!" Nicole called out, wrapping her arms around Maggie in a tight hug as she approached. Maggie smiled, a soft blush coloring her cheeks from the sudden attention.

If you keep this up," Maggie smirked, I may have to go away more often."

Jamie Preston strolled into the report room and snuck up behind Nicole, placing a hand on her shoulder as he looked over at Maggie. Welcome back, Maggie. I have to admit—I won t be missing this one here. All she does is talk, talk, talk."

He gave Nicole s shoulder a light squeeze to show he was kidding, then made his way to the coffee pot. Nicole and Maggie both laughed as the phone in the corner began to ring. Jamie picked it up, exchanged a quick word, and gestured to Nicole that the call was for her.

Maggie joined Jamie and poured herself a cup of coffee, glancing over at Nicole, who was now fidgeting as she spoke on the phone. A few tense moments passed before Nicole slammed the receiver down.

Shit!" she muttered, striding over to them.

What s going on? Everything okay?" Maggie asked, her brow furrowed.

"It's Gary. It's always Gary." Nicole rolled her eyes and looked away, clearly trying to hide her disgust. "I can't believe the crap he puts me through."

"Holy cow, I'm sorry," Jamie said, handing her a cup of coffee. "What's he doing now?"

"He needs money. He's stuck in Dallas—been up there all week. I'm so tired of this… I hung up on him! I already told him I'm through with him. No more."

She took a sip of the coffee, her hands trembling just slightly.

"I'm sorry, Nicole. I hope you stick with it and stay strong. Otherwise, this guy's just going to drag you down." Jamie offered her a firm nod. "Hey, I've gotta run. See you later." He waved to Maggie. "Remember—be strong, Nicole."

Nicole gave a tired sigh and turned to Maggie. "Let's get going. I've already picked up our keys," she said, holding them up with a little shake.

Within the first hour of their shift, they were dispatched to a boy's correctional facility. On the way, Maggie tried to strike up a conversation with Nicole, but it was clear her partner was distracted. She eventually gave up, letting the ride pass in silence. Thankfully, their friendship had grown to the point where silence wasn't awkward. Sometimes, it was even welcome. They respected each other's moods without needing explanation. Maggie knew Nicole would talk when she was ready—there was no need to push.

As the ambulance pulled up to the small brick building, Maggie noted the metal bars on the windows and the fifteen-foot perimeter fence topped with barbed wire. A security guard in a gray uniform stood waiting to escort them inside.

Despite knowing the dispatch was for a boy with an asthma attack, Maggie couldn't shake the unease curling in her stomach. Her thoughts drifted to the teenager who had died just weeks earlier from a gunshot wound in the mall parking lot. Working calls like these, especially in correctional facilities, always stirred up nerves. She knew the mix of violence and untreated behavioral issues could turn any situation unpredictable.

Nicole slid open the ambulance's side door and pulled out two medical bags while Maggie grabbed the stretcher and an oxygen tank.

"Right this way," said the gray-haired Hispanic guard, his voice tinged with an accent. They followed as he shuffled forward, slowly navigating the entryway. Twice he stopped, fumbling through a heavy key ring to unlock the doors.

"Got the right key here somewhere," he muttered each time.

Maggie fought the rising anxiety. If this were a true asthma attack, every second mattered. She just hoped they weren't too late.

Finally, they entered the gymnasium. About fifteen boys sat on the bleachers while two guards and a man in a business suit knelt beside a young boy lying on the floor. A sharp whistle pierced the air from somewhere in the bleachers, followed by snickers and mocking wisecracks from the other boys.

One of the boys hollered from the bleachers, "Hey baby, you can fix my broken heart anytime!"

Laughter erupted from the group until one of the guards snapped his wooden baton against the metal railing.

"Cut the noise! Keep it quiet!" he barked.

Nicole and Maggie ignored the jeering, not wanting to give the boys any reaction to feed off. They stayed focused.

"Great, you made it," said a man approaching them in business attire. "I'm Mike Horton, the facility director." He exhaled in relief as he offered a quick handshake. "This is Pete Morgan. He's thirteen. Has a history of asthma, but it's been a few years since his last attack. He was playing basketball and just suddenly couldn't breathe."

He stepped back, giving them room.

Nicole knelt beside the boy. Pete sat hunched forward, arms braced on his knees, his breathing shallow and wheezy. Maggie was already at work, pulling out the nasal cannula and connecting him to two liters of oxygen.

"What medications is he taking?" Nicole asked, eyes still scanning Pete's condition.

"I'm not sure," Mike admitted. "He's only been here a few days. I just know he's got a history."

Nicole nodded, listening to Pete's lungs with her stethoscope. "Tight wheezing in the upper lobes... barely any air movement in the lower. Maggie, do you have the nebulizer ready?"

Before Nicole could turn, Maggie tapped her shoulder, already holding the device. Nicole guided it gently to Pete's face.

"Hey, Pete," she said softly. "Are you taking any inhalers? Any medicine?"

The boy shook his head no, his eyes wide and anxious as he gripped the mask tightly over his nose and mouth, inhaling the aerosolized mist.

"Try to take slow, deep breaths. Let the medicine get down into your lungs, okay?" Nicole touched his hand lightly, offering reassurance. Pete gave a small nod, though his panic was evident.

Maggie prepped an IV bag and a catheter.

Pete, I need to take a look at your arm," she said. "We're going to start some more medication."

Pete extended his arm, trembling from the medication and fear. Maggie worked quickly, inserting the catheter while Nicole monitored vitals.

"His breathing's still too labored. He's going to tire out," Nicole said, rising. "Let's keep the treatment going en route. We need to move."

She pulled the stretcher closer, locking the wheels in place.

"Do you want to intubate before we leave?" Maggie asked, securing the IV line.

Nicole paused, eyeing Pete closely. His breathing was rough but still effective, for now.

"Not yet. Let's monitor him on the way. If he goes downhill, I'll intubate in the rig."

Maggie nodded, and together, they lifted Pete onto the stretcher. The sound in the gym faded as they focused only on the boy, the mist curling from the mask, the weight of his fear, and the urgency of every breath.

"If we put a tube in him and put him on a ventilator, he may have a hard time coming off," Nicole said firmly. "Let's just get him on some steroids and get him to the hospital."

Maggie nodded, helping lift Pete onto the stretcher and packing up their gear. As they worked, one of the guards stepped forward from the background.

"Does he really need to go to the hospital?" the younger guard asked, arms folded. His crisp, starched uniform looked freshly pressed, and he pushed his thick, black-framed glasses up the bridge of his nose with one finger. His other hand rested on his belt, close to his holster. "If he goes, I have to send one of my guys with you—and that means overtime."

Nicole turned to him, her expression hardening. "I'm sorry it's going to mess with your staffing, but this boy is very sick. And it didn't help that it took us forever to get through the front gate."

Without waiting for a reply, she and Maggie started wheeling Pete out. The younger guard gave a curt nod and motioned for the older Hispanic guard to accompany them. Then he turned and walked back toward the bleachers, resuming his oversight of the other boys.

They moved quickly, their pace brisk—so brisk that the older guard had to hurry to keep up, breathing hard behind them.

"I'm telling you, Maggie," Nicole muttered, "I need a vacation. Little comments like that overtime crap just push me over the edge."

"I know," Maggie said softly. "Just blow it off. It's not worth it."

She glanced over and caught the anguish in Nicole's eyes—more than frustration, it was exhaustion, emotional wear. But she didn't press. She knew better.

Maggie rode in the back with Pete while Nicole drove them to the University Hospital. The continuous nebulizer treatment was working—Pete's wheezing was easing, and the movement of air through his lungs was noticeably better by the time they pulled into the ER bay.

After giving their report to the hospital staff, they cleaned the stretcher and decided to treat themselves to a gourmet coffee while they waited for their next call. Just a short ten-minute drive brought them to I-10 and Huebner Oaks—a good central location with easy highway access if they got dispatched across town.

Maggie stayed in the ambulance while Nicole went inside for drinks. She sat quietly, gazing through the window, watching people walk in and out of the strip of clothing stores, their arms full of bags, smiles on their faces. The mundanity of their lives felt oddly comforting.

A sudden tap on the window startled her. She hadn't even seen Nicole return.

Nicole stood outside the passenger door, a muffin held between her teeth, two iced white chocolate mochas gripped in her hands, and a mess of napkins tucked under her arm.

Maggie rolled the window down, laughing as she reached for one of the cups.

"You are a sight," she said with a grin.

Nicole mumbled something unintelligible through the muffin, which only made Maggie laugh harder.

"Hey, you're pretty talented. Can you carry a few more things in your mouth like that? You didn't learn that from Wrangler, did you?" Maggie laughed at her own joke.

Nicole rolled her eyes as she handed over the coffee, then retrieved the muffin from her mouth with exaggerated care.

"Yeah, whatever. Next time you go in, and I'll sit out here looking all cute." She tossed a few napkins at Maggie, one of them bouncing off her forehead.

Nicole hopped into the driver's seat, still grinning. Maggie watched her for a moment, then spoke quietly.

"It's nice to see you smile. You've been... really upset lately."

Nicole hesitated, her fingers still wrapped around the steering wheel. "I'm sorry," she said softly. "Hey, let's keep things light for now. Tell me about your trip—sunshine, white sandy beaches, moonlight walks by the ocean—tell me!"

She turned to Maggie with a hopeful grin, trying to lift the moment.

Maggie looked down at her drink, slowly twirling the straw through the ice. It was okay."

Just okay? Are you nuts?" Nicole feigned offense. Next time, you stay here and cover shifts, and I'll go with Victor to paradise!"

Maggie gave a half-smile but kept her eyes on her drink.

Nicole's expression softened. Alright... on a more serious note. What's going on? You know you can talk to me."

She reached over, gently brushing Maggie's forearm with her fingers before pulling away, giving her space.

Maggie sighed and quickly wiped a tear from the corner of her eye. I don't know what's wrong with me," she said, voice barely above a whisper. I can't seem to make Victor happy. He gets angry over nothing. And I feel... so distant from him. I don't know what I'm doing wrong."

Nicole shook her head. First of all, let's get something straight—you are not doing anything wrong. Stop beating yourself up."

She paused, choosing her words carefully.

Maybe Victor's just stressed. The market's been all over the place lately; it could be a hundred things. I'm not saying it's okay for him to take it out on you. But maybe you two need to talk. Really talk. Or even see someone together."

Nicole glanced over, her heart sinking as she watched Maggie, still staring into her drink like it might offer some kind of answer. The pain in her friend's face cut deep, deeper than Nicole expected. She felt it like a punch to the chest.

She thought of Gary.

All the distractions, the way she'd been caught up in her own stress and hadn't seen how much Maggie was hurting. The guilt swelled in her throat.

"Maggie..." she began gently.

But Maggie raised a hand, cutting her off. "It's alright," she said quickly. "Let's change the subject."

She wiped away another tear and forced a smile, the kind that didn't quite reach her eyes.

Nicole nodded, though the sadness lingered between them like fog neither of them knew how to clear.

"What have I missed this last week?" Maggie finally looked toward Nicole, managing a faint smile.

"Not much, same old stuff," Nicole replied, tearing a piece of her muffin and offering it. "Want some?"

"No, I'm not hungry, thanks." Maggie paused, her expression shifting. "Any more rapes? That creepy guy... Butterfly, or whatever his signature was?"

Nicole's eyes narrowed slightly at the mention, but she kept her voice calm. "No, nothing recently. It's been pretty quiet."

"Maybe he's gone. Got bored?" Maggie asked, though her thoughts seemed elsewhere, perhaps still lingering in Dallas with Gary.

"I doubt it," Nicole said with a half-shrug. "Probably sitting in jail for some dumb parking ticket. He'll be out by next week."

"You're probably right," Maggie muttered, shaking her head.

The rest of their shift passed without much urgency. Maggie dozed in the passenger seat, her head resting against the window, legs stretched out toward Nicole. Nicole flipped through an investment magazine, but her attention often drifted to the woman asleep beside her.

She'd seen Maggie like this a hundred times, peaceful, vulnerable, beautiful. Even on Maggie's worst days, that beauty never seemed to fade. Nicole let her eyes linger before she gently closed them, letting her mind wander. Daydreams, familiar and bittersweet, crept in before she forced them back behind a sigh.

Why do I do this to myself? she wondered. Chasing a dream that isn't mine to have.

Part of her longed to meet someone—anyone—who might free her from the silent ache she carried. But the stronger part of her heart-the stubborn, loyal, ever-hopeful part just couldn't let go of Maggie, no matter how distant that hope had become.

About an hour before the end of their shift, dispatch crackled through the radio: "Unit 12, return to station."

Maggie stirred and stretched, her arm flopping sideways and playfully hitting Nicole on the ear.

"She's alive!" Nicole said in a monster voice, ducking with a grin.

"Wow... thanks for letting me sleep," Maggie said, brushing her hair back. "That felt great. I think I'm still fighting jet lag."

"Well, let's go," Nicole said, folding her magazine and starting the engine. "Wonder what the station wants."

"I don't know, but I'm ready to go home," Nicole murmured, her voice carrying a hint of exhaustion.

As they walked into the station, a woman with a young girl approached them, a warm smile on her face.

"Maggie... hello. I don't know if you remember us," the woman said. She was in her late thirties, with strawberry blonde hair neatly combed into a bun and bright blue eyes. She wore a server uniform, and beside her, the little girl stood, holding a plate wrapped in foil.

Maggie paused and squinted, recognition slowly dawning on her face. "Yes... I remember you," she said, her smile softening as she looked down at the girl. "Jill, right? How are you?"

The little girl shyly hid behind her mother's leg, her bright blue eyes peeking out as she gave a quiet, "Fine."

Maggie knelt down, brushing a lock of hair away from Jill's face. "Look at you, so grown up! You're getting bigger every time I see you," Maggie said, smiling with warmth as Jill handed her the plate.

The woman's voice faltered as she spoke. "Jill and I wanted to come see you today. We baked you some cookies. It's been one year since the accident, and we wanted to let you know there's not a day that goes by that we don't think of you. We are so grateful for the strength and compassion you showed us."

Maggie's expression softened. "Thank you," she said quietly, pulling the woman into a gentle hug. "I'm just glad everything turned out all right. I truly believe in angels... and they were watching out for us that night. Look at her," Maggie said, her voice laced with amazement. "She looks amazing. Thanks to you, especially."

Maggie turned her attention to Jill. "Jill wanted to give you this picture. I hope it's okay. I brought it to work, but my schedule's been so hectic. I tried to get off today but couldn't."

The woman handed Maggie a drawing, and Maggie's eyes softened. "This is fine. It's so nice to see you both doing so well."

"Well, I better get going. I need to drop Jill off at my mom s and get to work. Thank you again for everything... for being so kind. You re a special person," the woman said, wrapping Maggie in another hug.

Maggie bent down to hug Jill goodbye, watching them walk away with a bittersweet smile. Nicole, who had stood quietly in the background, approached as they left.

What was that all about?" Nicole asked with curiosity in her tone.

Maggie s smile turned wistful as she watched the pair leave. Basically, a miracle child. I still can t believe how well she did." She paused, gathering her thoughts. I was driving back into town from Kerrville on I-10. They were in front of me, about fifty feet ahead. The rain was pouring, and the mom lost control of her car. The Blazer swerved and flipped about five times. I was behind them in my BMW, the first responder."

Her voice faltered for a moment as the memory played out in her mind. I was terrified. I didn t have my first aid kit or anything with me. The mom was still strapped in, with a broken arm and cuts all over, but Jill... she fell out. The seatbelt must ve snapped, and she flew out of the passenger window as the car rolled. Her little body was twisted, and I had to do CPR for almost fifteen minutes before I could get her heart beating again."

Nicole's face shifted to a look of awe. And EMS arrived just in time?"

Yeah. They couldn t fly her out because of the weather, so we intubated her and got her to the University. By the time they got her cleaned up, no internal injuries. They took her off the ventilator the next day. She was discharged two days later. Talk about a lucky little girl."

Nicole's voice was proud, her gaze fixed on Maggie with admiration. "So the mom was right. If it weren't for you, Jill might not have made it."

Maggie looked away for a moment, her emotions settling into quiet humility. "I was just doing what I had to do. I'm glad I was there, though. Glad I could help."

"You know, when I think about it, it was about 10 minutes before the next car arrived to help. The mom couldn't get to Jill, so maybe I was just supposed to be there at that specific time... that right moment?" Maggie said, a touch of cocky confidence in her voice as she smiled.

Nicole looked at her and placed a gentle arm around Maggie's shoulders. "It feels good, doesn't it?"

"Yes, it does. Thank you," Maggie replied, her smile softening with gratitude.

The next day, Maggie and Nicole arrived late to the break room, and the other three teams were already seated around the table. The shift leader was handing out packets, and one of the paramedics waved for Maggie and Nicole to sit with him.

Maggie leaned over and tugged on Nicole's arm, a teasing grin spreading across her face. "Well, hello, Johnny," she whispered under her breath, letting out a small laugh.

Nicole rolled her eyes but smiled. "Stop, you better be good."

Maggie's grin only widened as Nicole took the seat next to Johnny. He leaned back in his chair, his trademark cocky smile flashing as he greeted her. "Hey, gorgeous. It's nice to see you. Where have you been lately?"

"I've been alright. I'll talk to you after the meeting," Nicole replied, briefly touching his arm before redirecting her attention to the shift leader.

Johnny had gone to paramedic school with Nicole, and they d both started working for the city around the same time. His flirtatious nature was well-known, and he d made his moves on more than a few of the women in the department. But Nicole was a different story. While she could admit there was a certain chemistry between them, she wasn t easily swayed by his charm.

Johnny s Latino charisma was magnetic—his dark brown eyes, jet-black hair, and slim but strong frame always seemed to draw attention. There was something about the hint of scruff on his face, the casual but debonair way he carried himself, that made him a constant presence in her thoughts. He was an avid bike rider and often hosted charity events for sick children; his enthusiasm was always infectious. Yet despite the countless flirtations, Nicole was unsure if Johnny was still pursuing her for the thrill of the chase or if he, too, felt something deeper. She hadn t been that interested in many men, but Johnny was one of the few who had caught her attention.

As the meeting came to a close, Nicole began to stand up, but Johnny s hand gently pulled her back into her seat, closer to him. His smile was disarming, full of intrigue. So, are you hiding from me on purpose?"

Nicole looked into his dark eyes and gave a small, amused smile. You ll have to wait and find out." She was about to get up again when Maggie turned around to leave.

Hello to you, too!" Maggie called out, giving Johnny a playful grin.

Johnny chuckled, looking at Maggie with an apologetic smile. Hi, Maggie. Sorry. It s like you ve got an off-limits sign on your forehead."

Maggie rolled her eyes but couldn t help laughing. Yeah, right! When does married mean off-limits to any man?" She winked at Nicole before turning to walk away. I ll meet you outside, Nicole."

"Touchy," Johnny teased, resting his arm on the back of Nicole's chair and leaning in closer.

Nicole smirked, not missing a beat. "I've just been busy these days. What about you? Spending time with your kids?"

Johnny's expression softened, his usual flirtation giving way to something more genuine. "Yeah, I've been trying to. Family stuff, you know? But I can always make time for you," he added with a wink.

Nicole chuckled, though there was an underlying tension in the air, one that neither of them could deny.

"Yeah, they're getting big," Johnny said.

"Before you know it, you'll be a grandpa," Maggie teased, trying to lighten the moment.

"I'll be knocking some heads against the wall if that happens," Johnny remarked.

Just then, Mike, the shift supervisor, walked up, glancing at the scene. "Hey, is he sexually harassing you? Cause if not, I think I will," Mike joked, shaking Johnny's hand firmly. "Hey, buddy."

Johnny laughed. "How's it going, Mike? We almost missed the meeting today, but you kept us busy out there."

Mike nodded, his tone turning more serious. "I know, we've been busy lately... Lots of overtime..." he hinted. "Well, boys, it's back to the grind. Maggie's waiting; we've still got a few more hours on shift." He clapped Johnny on the shoulder. "It's good to see you guys."

Johnny rose, gave Nicole a brief hug, then sank back into his seat beside Mike.

"Okay...I'll catch you later." Nicole grabbed her things and began leaving.

As Nicole walked toward the ambulance, Maggie met her at the door.

"Hey, we just got another call. I was coming to get you." Maggie tossed the keys to Nicole as they hurried back to the vehicle. "Where to?"

"Italian restaurant on Houston Street downtown," Maggie replied.

"Too bad I already ate. I like that restaurant—have you eaten there before?"

"No, I haven't," Maggie answered, climbing into the passenger seat as Nicole started the engine.

The ambulance pulled into a narrow driveway, and a police officer gestured for them to follow him to the back of the restaurant. They parked and grabbed their equipment, weaving through a crowd of officers until they reached the scene.

Maggie's gaze drifted up to the streetlight overhead, its bright glow attracting hundreds of buzzing insects. She then turned her attention to the couple on the ground—Jake Miller, the man holding his wife, Claire, who was draped in a blanket.

"My wife... she's got a deep laceration on her forehead. No broken bones or anything, but we need to clean and suture the wound to minimize scarring," Jake said, stepping back to give Maggie and Nicole room to work.

Maggie gently took over holding the bandage on Claire's forehead while the man stood up. "And you are?" she asked.

"Jake Miller. I'm an ER doctor from Detroit. My wife, Claire, and I are on our honeymoon. I don't understand how this could've happened. She was only a minute ahead of me."

Claire, still visibly shaken, reached for Jake. "Honey, it's okay. You stopped it from happening. I'm just sorry I went ahead," she said, her voice quivering as tears welled in her eyes.

Maggie continued her work, securing the bandage with tape. "It's going to be okay. We'll take you to the hospital. You're in good hands."

Nicole helped Claire onto the stretcher, and just as they were about to load her into the ambulance, Detective Mallory arrived.

"Dr. Miller, I'm Detective Mallory. I'll need to get some information from you." Mallory offered Jake his hand. "Mrs. Reed, do you have room for me to ride along, or would you prefer Dr. Miller to come with me?"

Jake immediately interrupted. "No, I want to stay with my wife."

"You can ride with us," Maggie said, giving him a reassuring smile as she allowed Jake and Mallory to board the ambulance.

Inside the ambulance, Maggie checked Claire's vital signs and replaced the bandage on her forehead with a fresh sterile pad. Detective Mallory opened his notepad, his voice steady and professional.

"Did you see the man who pulled you into the alley between the buildings?" Mallory asked Claire.

Claire's voice trembled as she spoke. "It happened so fast. While Jake went to the restroom, I told him I'd meet him outside. I was just leaning against the car, enjoying the nice weather, and then this man pulled me into the alley. He hit me... or something. I think I blacked out for a moment. It all happened so quickly."

Maggie placed a comforting hand on Claire's shoulder, keeping her calm. "You're doing great, Claire. We'll get you the care you need."

Mallory turned his attention to Jake. Did you see anything unusual? Anything at all?"

Jake shook his head. I came out of the restaurant, looked around for Claire, and then I heard her screaming. The guy let her go and ran off. I didn't see his face, but he had a jean jacket and a baseball cap. That's all I could make out. I didn't chase him—I stayed with Claire."

Mallory nodded. You did the right thing, Dr. Miller. Claire, did the man say anything to you?"

Claire wiped away a tear, her voice shaky. I don't remember hearing anything… it was like everything was muffled, a blur. I wish I could tell you more."

The ambulance finally arrived at the hospital. Maggie quickly jumped out, helping the team unload Claire. As Jake followed, Mallory handed him a business card.

Thank you for your cooperation," Mallory said. If you remember anything else, don't hesitate to call."

Jake tucked the card into his shirt pocket as they rolled Claire through the emergency room doors. Maggie gave a report to the ER nurse before saying her goodbyes to the Millers.nBack in the ambulance, Nicole was cleaning up the unit. She looked up as Maggie climbed in. So… was it the same guy who attacked the other women?"

Maggie sighed, leaning against the wall as she filed the paperwork. I don't know. Claire was really shaken up and couldn't remember much. It's just so sad… what a way to spend your honeymoon."

Nicole shook her head, a knowing look in her eyes. They should've picked the Cayman Islands."

Maggie smiled faintly. Probably." She paused for a moment, the weight of the case lingering. I hope she's okay."

CHAPTER FOURTEEN

The heavy oak door creaked open. Dr. Webster stepped halfway out and held up a hand, signaling Victor to wait as he finished a conversation inside. Victor remained seated in the modest waiting area, fidgeting restlessly. He reached for a magazine on the table, flipping through the pages without reading—just looking at the pictures.

From his seat, Victor could see Dr. Webster, though the man he was speaking to remained out of view. He tried not to stare, but his unease only grew as the muffled voices continued. Eventually, he tossed the magazine back onto the table with a soft slap and shifted in his chair.

The conversation ended, and the other man stepped into view, walking toward the door. As he passed, his eyes met Victor s—and for a brief moment, time seemed to slow. Victor recognized him instantly. Detective Mallory. He had seen him on the news more than once.

Victor, sorry to keep you waiting," Dr. Webster said warmly, stepping forward and extending a hand.

Victor stood and shook it. As he followed Dr. Webster into the office, he shot one last glance toward the exit, half-expecting Detective Mallory to come back through the door.

So," Dr. Webster began, moving behind his desk. It s been a few weeks. Tell me, how have things been with you?"

Victor took a seat on the familiar couch, placing his hands on his knees, then crossing his arms over his chest. Everything s going well... well, except the stock market." He smiled faintly, though it didn t reach his eyes.

Dr. Webster studied him, pausing as he picked up his pipe and placed the mouthpiece between his lips. You seem a little tense. Is everything all right?"

I m fine," Victor said quickly. Just need some more sleep. Still feeling a little jet-lagged."

Ah, yes. The trip," Dr. Webster said, finding his lighter. I was there with my wife two summers ago. Beautiful place." He lit the pipe, inhaled deeply, and exhaled a slow, thick cloud of smoke. The scent of tobacco filled the room, warm and earthy.

It was a good trip," Victor said. Maggie and I needed it."

A pause. Then he asked, more casually than he felt, Hey... wasn t that a detective who was just in here? I m sure I ve seen him on the news a few times."

Dr. Webster exhaled another puff, nodding slowly. Yes. Detective Mallory. He s working on a case and asked for a professional opinion."

Victor didn t press further, but something in his jaw tightened.

Dr. Webster opened his leather-bound notebook and crossed one leg over the other. Let s see," he said thoughtfully. Today, I d like to try hypnotics again. It s been a while, hasn t it?"

Victor nodded, already shifting his posture.

Good. Why don t you lay back, take a few breaths, and try to relax," Dr. Webster said, his tone softening. We ll talk a little... and then we ll begin."

Victor slid back into the leather sofa, resting his head on a pillow. Dr. Webster moved to the window and slowly turned the blinds shut, dimming the room. After ten minutes of guided relaxation, Victor slipped into a deep hypnotic state. Dr. Webster spoke in a low, soothing voice, leading him through the usual prompts. Victor responded calmly at first, but as they neared a familiar threshold, something buried deep in his agitation began to rise. His breathing quickened. His hands clenched. As in previous sessions, once that invisible wall was reached, everything unraveled.

His heart rate spiked, and his breath became labored. Dr. Webster gently ended the session. He let Victor rest while he scribbled notes into a thick folder on his lap.

"Feeling better now?" he asked, nudging his glasses up his nose.

Victor sat up slowly, leaning forward, his elbows resting on his knees. He pressed his face into his palms. "Yeah... I'm fine. These sessions drain me."

"We keep hitting the same block," Dr. Webster said quietly. "A point in your childhood you seem determined to avoid. I believe you're suppressing something important—something your mind is protecting."

"I'm not sure," Victor muttered, his eyes distant, unfocused.

Dr. Webster closed the folder with a soft thud and adjusted his glasses again, his expression tinged with frustration. "I'll think on it. Maybe next week we can try a different method. There has to be a way through."

He stood and extended a hand.

Victor shook it without much thought. "Sure. Maybe better luck next time."

Dr. Webster watched him walk out the door, his posture thoughtful. Something about Victor's flat tone lingered. He let out another troubled sigh. Victor arrived home to the muffled clatter of tools and the faint echo of barking. As he stepped into the kitchen, Wrangler's bark startled Maggie, who was half beneath the kitchen sink with yellow gloves on her hands. She jerked upward, bumping her head against the cabinet with a soft thunk.

"Dammit—" she muttered, then looked up and caught sight of Victor.

She had grease smeared across one cheek, her shirt dusted with cleaning residue, and her sleeves pushed past her elbows. Her hair was pulled back beneath a blue and white bandana, slightly damp from exertion. She gave him a tired smile, still crouched on one knee, a dirty rag in one hand.

"My gosh, you scared me," she said with a laugh. "This is a mess. You want to help?"

Victor smiled faintly, but his eyes betrayed something deeper—something still stuck in that dark place he couldn't reach.

"No thanks, I think I'll pass on that offer. What's for dinner?"

"Pizza... or, if you're feeling adventurous, you could cook," she teased, smiling.

"Sounds like a pizza night. I'll order it after I take a shower," Victor said, already turning toward the hallway.

"Hey..." Maggie called out. "I brought a box down from the attic when I was putting some junk away. Is it yours? It has a lock on it. I don't remember seeing it before."

Victor stopped in his tracks. He hesitated, then turned around.

"Yeah, that's mine. Just some old stuff."

"How come the lock? You hiding something?" she asked playfully.

It s nothing. Why all the questions? Can t I have some privacy?" Victor snapped. His voice rose without warning, and he slammed his hand against the wall. Startled, Maggie took a step back. Victor stormed over, snatched the locked box from the cabinet, and headed upstairs.

Damn it, just leave my things alone!" His voice echoed down the stairwell.

Maggie remained kneeling on the floor, staring at the empty doorway where Victor had just stood. She dropped the damp cloth, then placed a trembling hand on her forehead, eyes closed. Her chest tightened, her heart pounding. Tears welled in her eyes.

She slowly stood, yanked off the yellow gloves, and tossed them to the floor. Without saying another word, she grabbed her purse and keys and walked out the front door.

Before she even realized where she was going, Maggie was already in the car, hands clenched on the steering wheel, her mind spiraling. She pulled over on the side of the road and leaned forward, pressing her forehead against the wheel. A sob escaped her lips, then another, until the dam broke and she cried uncontrollably.

After a while, her sobs quieted. She wiped her face with her sleeve and stared out the windshield. The moon glimmered on the wet pavement—it had started to rain. She reached for the visor and flipped it down, glancing at herself in the mirror. Her eyes were puffy, red, and tired. The grease from earlier still smeared one cheek, a reminder of the ordinary day that had just shattered.

She shook her head and started driving again.

Maggie pulled her black BMW up in front of Nicole s house. For a few seconds, she just sat there, staring at the warmly lit apartment above. If anyone could see her like this, it was Nicole. She had been there before—

on a worse night, in the rain, covered in blood, no makeup, no pride. If anyone understood, it was her.

Maggie stepped out into the cool night, climbing the front steps just as Nicole's neighbor, Minnie, opened the door to let out her two cocker spaniels.

The dogs immediately darted over, circling Maggie's legs, sniffing with excitement, their short tails wagging furiously.

"Hey, Bonnie and Clyde," she said, crouching down and petting them as they whimpered and yipped happily. The touch of fur and warmth grounded her, even if just for a moment.

"Maggie, my dear, how are you?" Minnie asked kindly. She paused, noticing Maggie's red, swollen eyes. It was clear she had been crying.

"Oh, I'm fine. I was hoping to catch my partner in crime at home this evening. I wanted to go over some stuff with her about work," Maggie replied, attempting a small smile.

"Yes, my dear, she's home. Have her share some of the casserole I sent up earlier tonight—if she hasn't already eaten it all," Minnie chuckled.

"Go right along now, don't mind me. I'm just taking these two little rascals for a walk, or they'll never let me get any sleep," she added as she shuffled past in her pink, fluffy slippers, her two cocker spaniels trotting happily by her side.

Maggie watched them waddle down the sidewalk, then turned and walked inside, heading up the staircase to Nicole's apartment.

Nicole answered the door in blue flannel pajama bottoms and a white tee shirt, her hair freshly combed back and still damp.

Hey, what a surprise," she smiled. "I just got out of the shower. What brings you over to my side of the woods?"

Maggie stepped inside, glancing around the cozy apartment. She had only been there a few times before. The walls were painted a soft green with clean white trim, giving the space a calming, elegant feel. Mahogany wood framed much of the room's furnishings, and Nicole's love of art was evident in the carefully curated, framed pieces throughout the space.

"Ahh... nothing feels better than a hot shower after working out," Nicole said, sitting down on the couch and pulling on her socks.

Maggie walked over and sat beside her.

Nicole paused, finally noticing the wear in Maggie's face—the redness around her eyes, the heaviness in her expression.

"Is everything all right?" she asked, concern creeping into her voice.

"I'm sorry for bothering you," Maggie said, her voice cracking. "I just didn't have anywhere else to go. I can't take this anymore. Victor's behavior—one minute he's fine, then the next he's angry and yelling for no reason at all." Tears streamed down her face.

"Hey, hey... it's okay. Come here," Nicole said gently, scooting closer and wrapping her arms around her.

"And you're no bother," she added softly. "You know you can come here anytime. I mean it—you always have a place to go."

Maggie closed her eyes and rested her head on Nicole's shoulder, letting the tears fall. Nicole leaned back into the couch, supporting her, letting her melt into the embrace.

"Can you just... hold me?" Maggie whispered through tears. "I just want you to hold me."

"Sure. Just rest. I'll stay with you," Nicole replied, reaching over to turn off the lamp beside them. In the dim silence, she gently placed her hand on the back of Maggie's head, stroking her hair until her breathing slowed and she fell asleep.

Maggie awoke slowly, her eyelids heavy and sticky from dried tears. For a moment, she forgot where she was—until she realized her head was still against Nicole's chest. Nicole had fallen asleep, her head tilted back, mouth slightly open.

Maggie glanced at the clock: 2:00 a.m.

She hesitated, not wanting to move. It felt warm and safe in Nicole's arms—comforting in a way she hadn't felt in a long time. The faint scent of fabric softener still lingered in Nicole's shirt, wrapping Maggie in a clean, quiet peace.

After a few more minutes, she gently eased herself up. She grabbed a pillow from the couch and placed it next to Nicole's head, then pulled a soft blanket over her. Leaning down, she kissed Nicole's forehead.

"Thank you," she whispered.

The streets were nearly empty as Maggie drove home. Her mind drifted back to Victor. Her chest ached. She wanted to cry again, but couldn't summon the strength.

She pulled into the empty garage—Victor's truck wasn't there.

Inside, the house was quiet. Maggie slipped off her shoes, walked to the bedroom, and curled up on the bed. Her dog, Wrangler, jumped up beside her, settling in close.

Within moments, they were both fast asleep.

CHAPTER FIFTEEN

Clouds churned in gray and black swirls, masking the sun behind a dense, oppressive sky. The wind howled through the trees, bending them in protest as fat raindrops splattered the ground below. It felt as though the heavens had saved all their sorrow for this day. In San Antonio, heavy rain turned ordinary drives into deadly gambles. Low water crossings, clearly marked and well-known, still claimed lives each year—drivers misjudging their depth or overestimating their own luck. Maggie knew the risks all too well.

As she and Nicole arrived at the scene, a police officer directing traffic motioned for them to stop. Rain pounded on his hat, water streaming steadily off the brim as he leaned toward the ambulance's driver-side window. Nicole rolled it down.

Where do you want us?" she asked, her eyes scanning the scene beyond the windshield. Several squad cars lined the parking lot, and officers—some in uniform, others in plainclothes—gathered near a field bordering a wooded area.

Her body s over there," the officer said, pointing. It d be best if you waited in your rig on that side. I ll call you if we need anything."

The plastic poncho covering him flapped wildly in the wind as he turned and jogged back to the intersection to continue directing traffic.

Nicole nodded and rolled the window up, then parked the ambulance within clear view of the scene. Maggie leaned forward, watching through the rain-streaked glass. Officers stood in the downpour, unmoved by the weather, some smoking as they waited for orders. Her eyes settled on Detective Mallory, who was speaking with a man near the body. Maggie's stomach tensed.

Could this be another victim of the serial rapist?

"What do you think? You think it's the same guy who raped those other women?" Maggie asked, still watching the men gathered outside.

"I don't know," Nicole replied, leaning her head back against the seat. "But I'm sure glad we're not out there with them."

A buzzing sound came from her jacket pocket. Nicole pulled out her phone and flipped open the tiny headset.

"Hello?" she said curtly.

Maggie glanced at her as Nicole's tone shifted.

"I said no, Gary. And I mean it. Don't come by. It's over—I'm not picking up your pieces anymore, so don't call me!"

She snapped the phone closed and shoved it back in her pocket.

"Bravo," Maggie said, reaching over to touch Nicole's shoulder. "I'm glad you're staying away from him. What happened this time?"

"Same crap," Nicole muttered, staring out the window. "But I'm through with him. This time, I mean it."

"Good for you. And hey... thanks for the other night. For being such a good friend. I don't know what I'd do without you."

Maggie leaned over and kissed Nicole gently on the cheek. Nicole's cheeks flushed pink, but she smiled.

As long as you re doing all right," Nicole said softly.

A sudden knock on the window startled them both.

It s cleared. You can go now," the officer said.

Nicole rolled up the window, started the engine, and eased the ambulance away from the scene. Maggie turned toward the passenger-side window, her gaze following the blur of rain-soaked figures moving through the gray haze. What a dreary day. The sky had darkened to a heavier shade of charcoal, and streetlights now glowed faintly, casting halos through the falling rain.

By the end of their shift, the downpour had eased into a steady mist. Maggie drove home in silence, her body weary and her heart heavy. She massaged her scalp absentmindedly with her fingernails, her elbow resting on the door. The rhythmic squeak of the windshield wipers filled the quiet space, a backdrop to her drifting thoughts. As she turned into her driveway, waiting for the garage door to rise, something caught her eye. A shadow, faint, but there, behind a tree at the side of the house. Maggie s body tensed. She hadn t been paying close attention, and the darkness made it hard to be sure… but she could have sworn someone was there.

Her heartbeat quickened.

Victor s truck was in the garage, and the lights inside the house were off. Maggie stayed in her car, watching the rearview mirror until the garage door fully closed behind her. Only then did she exhale. Enclosed in the safety of her home, she finally allowed herself to breathe. She stepped into the kitchen and flipped on the light. Her eyes immediately darted toward the sliding glass door. Drawn by instinct, she moved quickly across the room and locked the handle, pressing her face close to the glass as she peered into the rain-soaked night.

Her breath caught in her throat.

A man stood just feet away on the other side of the glass.

He didn't move. His jacket hood was pulled low over his head, shielding him from the rain. The shadows cloaked his features, but his presence was unmistakable.

Maggie's body froze. Her breath stilled. Her mind screamed, *Move!*, but her limbs wouldn't obey. Her heart pounded so hard she feared he might hear it. She spun around the corner, pressing her back to the wall, hidden from view. Panic clamped down on her chest like a vice. Was it Gary? The figure had looked familiar—something in the stance, the shape—but it had happened too quickly to be sure.

Why would he be here? She thought. *Why would he come to my house?*

Still gasping for air, she finally managed to peek back around the corner.

The man was gone.

She scanned the backyard—nothing but darkness and falling rain. Her muscles trembled. Her knees buckled, and she slid to the floor, her back pressed to the wall. Hugging her knees to her chest, she buried her chin in her arms and stayed there, frozen in fear.

It looked like Gary. She thought it was him. But she didn't *know*. Minutes passed—how many, she wasn't sure—before she finally got up and crept to the bedroom. She didn't turn on a light. She undressed in the dark, her hands shaking, and slipped beneath the covers beside Victor. For a moment, she considered waking him.

But she didn't. Her body still trembled. She didn't know if it was the chill from the rain or the encounter with the man outside, or the uncertainty of not knowing who he was.

She stared into the darkness, wide-eyed, too afraid to sleep.

CHAPTER SIXTEEN

Nicole McBride?" the man asked as he approached the table where Nicole sat.

She lowered the newspaper, peering up at him. It only took a moment to recognize the familiar face—Detective Mallory. Folding the paper, she gave a small wave to the server for more coffee.

Yes, I'm Nicole," she said, curiosity tightening her voice.

Good morning," he replied, slipping a badge from his coat just long enough to flash it. Detective Mallory, San Antonio Crime Division. I spoke with your neighbor, Minnie. She mentioned you might be here. Mind if I join you for a moment?"

Nicole gestured toward the seat across from her. Of course. Please, sit. Coffee's on the way. What's this about?"

Her first instinct was panic—her thoughts went straight to Gary.

I'm actually looking for your brother," Mallory said as he sat. When was the last time you saw him?"

Has he done something?" Nicole asked, brows knitting.

We're not certain yet. We just have a few questions for him."

From his coat pocket, Mallory pulled out a photograph and slid it across the table. "Have you ever seen this woman before—maybe with your brother?"

Nicole studied the picture. It was a school portrait—an old photo of the young woman found murdered in the alley, the same woman Gary had assaulted just days earlier. She knew it instantly, but hesitated.

Lifting her coffee cup, she took a slow sip to buy time, the hot liquid scorching her throat.

"I don't think so," she said finally, her voice even. "I've been trying to keep some distance from Gary. He's... always in need. Always getting into something."

She realized how it sounded and backpedaled slightly.

"I mean, not anything illegal. Just... money problems. You know."

Her hand trembled slightly as she set the cup down. She hated the part of Gary that pulled people into chaos. But still—he was her brother. And despite everything, some small, stubborn part of her still wanted to protect him.

"Do you know where I might find him?" Detective Mallory asked, eyeing Nicole sharply over the rim of his coffee cup.

Nicole shook her head. "No. I haven't seen him in a while."

Mallory didn't press immediately. He leaned back, watching her for a beat before shifting the conversation.

"I've seen you at a few of the crime scenes," he said casually. "With your paramedic partner."

"Maggie," Nicole replied, instinctively.

"Right. Mrs. Reed. You're usually the one driving, and she's in the back."

Nicole offered a small nod. The shift in topic didn't ease her nerves. If anything, his calm demeanor made her feel more exposed.

"It seems like we've been nonstop lately—car accidents, rapes... Honestly, I don't know which one we respond to more these days." Her voice was steady, but her hands fidgeted around her coffee cup.

Mallory gave a curt nod, eyes narrowing slightly. "Well, rest assured—we're going to find whoever's behind this."

He stood and slid a business card across the table. "If you hear from Gary—or know where he is—give me a call."

Nicole picked up the card slowly. "If I see him, I'll call you," she said, the lie passing her lips with practiced ease.

Mallory didn't say anything more. As he turned, he glanced at a message on his pager, his expression unreadable as he walked away.

Nicole sat motionless, staring at the card in her hand. Her thoughts flashed to the night she found Gary in that alley, fists flying in rage, the girl crying and bloodied on the pavement. The photograph Mallory had shown her was of that same girl, only younger, her face still untouched by the life that would later devour her.

A sick, sinking feeling took hold in Nicole's stomach. She slipped the card into her back pocket and closed her eyes, guilt washing over her in waves. She had lied. To protect her brother. A part of her hated him, but another part still couldn't let go. Couldn't let him face this alone. Not yet.

"More coffee?"

Nicole opened her eyes to find the waiter beside her. She forced a brittle smile.

"No, thank you. Just the check, please."

Feeling restless and frustrated, Nicole made her way downtown to the River Walk. When the punching bag wasn't enough, walking among strangers gave her a different kind of release. Something about blending into a crowd soothed her—no expectations, no judgment. The River Walk, with its winding cobblestone paths and bustling energy, was perfect for that.

She had walked these paths many times before, losing herself among the streams of tourists, locals, street performers, and shopkeepers. Nestled below the main downtown streets, the river snaked through a world of its own. As daylight faded into evening, nightclub lights blinked to life, drawing in college kids, military men, and professionals looking to unwind.

Nicole wandered until she reached a quiet spot off the beaten path—a tucked-away bar down a narrow alley near the business district. The crowd here was older, more subdued. It wasn't a tourist magnet, and that's what she liked about it.

She pushed open the door and scanned the room. Familiar faces, dim lighting and music, low enough to think. Paul was behind the bar, just where she'd left him months ago.

"Hey, Paul," Nicole greeted with a small smile, sliding into a stool at the far end.

Paul looked up and chuckled. "Well, look what the cat dragged in. Back from the dead, stranger."

He was built like a linebacker, thick with muscle and more hair than seemed possible. Nicole always noticed his hands—the thick, coarse hair above and below his knuckles made her shiver a bit. But for all his lumbering presence, Paul was gentle to the core—a teddy bear in a bartender's apron.

Still around," she said. "Just busy with work, life... the usual. What about you?"

Before Paul could answer, a stumbling drunk at the far end of the bar caught his attention. "Hey, buster—take it outside if you're gonna puke. I'm not cleaning up your mess again." He waved the man off, then turned back to Nicole, wiping down the bar in front of her.

"Sorry. Occupational hazard." He paused, glancing at her more closely. "Speaking of drunks... how's that brother of yours?"

Nicole froze for a second. The words hit harder than he meant them to. She forced a tight smile, her fingers curling slightly around her glass.

"He's... still finding new ways to cause trouble."

Paul nodded, sensing more behind her words but not pushing. "Well, tell him if he ends up here again drunk off his ass, he's sleeping in the alley."

Nicole gave a soft laugh, though the weight in her chest didn't lift. "I'll pass along the message."

With a deep sigh, Nicole murmured, "I guess he's all right. I haven't seen him in a few days. I've had enough of his crap, honestly. Have you seen him around?"

Paul nodded, his expression shifting to something between concern and resignation. "Yeah. Last week. He looked trashed. Had scrapes on his face—probably from falling down drunk. You're doing the right thing, Nic. Cutting him off. Don't let his mess weigh you down. It's not your burden to carry." He paused, then offered gently, "Hey—what'll you have to drink?"

Nicole hesitated, then stood. "You know, I thought I wanted a beer... but I think I just need sleep more."

Paul tilted his head slightly, studying her. "You sure you're okay?"

"Yeah," she said, forcing a small smile. "I'm fine. Really. I'll catch you later. Nice seeing you, Paul."

"Anytime, kiddo," he said softly as she turned to leave.

Nicole stepped back out into the cool night, the quiet pressing in around her. She made her way home, her footsteps slower than usual, like the weight of her thoughts had settled into her bones.

At home, she undressed and ran a hot bath, letting the steam fill the bathroom. She sank into the water, hoping it would wash away the tension coiled in her chest, but the worry didn't leave. The image of her brother's face lingered in her mind. The photo of the girl. Detective Mallory's voice. The lies she told.

Later, wrapped in her comforter, Nicole lay awake in the darkness. Her thoughts wouldn't stop spinning—Gary, the detective, the dead girl in the photo, the way the past kept creeping back.

Finally, she reached into her nightstand and pulled out a prescription bottle. She didn't take them often, but tonight felt different, heavy. She swallowed a pill, her fingers trembling slightly as she set the bottle back in the drawer.

Eventually, the medication pulled her into a restless sleep—one where the lines between fear, guilt, and love blurred into shadow.

CHAPTER SEVENTEEN

As the ambulance pulled into the convenience store parking lot, a uniformed police officer motioned for Maggie and Nicole to park on the far side of the building. With a sharp gesture, he signaled for them to wait.

Maggie scanned the scene. Several officers, weapons drawn, were pressed against the storefront wall, peering cautiously through the windows. Behind the counter, a young employee in a green uniform bearing the store's logo cowered with her hands over her ears. She looked terrified, her shoulders shaking with sobs.

In the aisles, a man waved a handgun erratically, shouting incoherently as he paced back and forth. Shelves were in disarray—boxes, bottles, and bags scattered across the floor where he had knocked them down in his frenzy. Occasionally, he stopped to glance out the window, muttering as if to someone only he could hear.

The officers stayed low, maintaining cover and observation. For nearly an hour, tense negotiations unfolded. Finally, the man dropped the weapon and slumped against the wall, his body drained of all fight.

Police rushed in, subduing him quickly. One officer kicked the gun out of reach while two others pinned him to the floor. Only then did the extent of the chaos inside become fully visible.

Blood was smeared across the tiles and shelves, spattering the walls. The man, it turned out, had broken bottles with his bare hands during his outburst and hadn't registered the severity of his injuries. Deep gashes lined his arms, and crimson streaked his clothing.

A nearby officer waved Maggie and Nicole inside once the scene was secured.

They moved swiftly, grabbing their gear and rolling the stretcher through the shattered entrance. As they entered, two officers remained on the ground, holding the man in place. His breathing was erratic, but he no longer resisted—his energy spent, his eyes distant.

"It wasn't even loaded," one officer muttered, peering into the barrel of the .38 Special he'd picked up off the floor.

"Well, that's good to know," Nicole replied, her voice tight with sarcasm.

Suddenly, the man beneath them stirred. Realizing he was restrained, he began thrashing, trying to fight off the two officers holding him down. Nicole and Maggie instinctively stepped back, giving the officers room to handle him.

"If you can keep him still, I'll sedate him," Maggie said, reaching into her trauma bag. She popped the cap off a syringe with her teeth, then punctured the rubber top of a vial of Ativan. As the officers pinned the man, Maggie swiped an alcohol pad across his upper arm and swiftly injected the medication.

Within minutes, the man's muscles slackened, his fight subsiding as the drug took effect. Nicole and Maggie moved in, quickly bandaging the cuts on his hands and arms and controlling the bleeding. Once stabilized, they secured him onto the stretcher. An officer snapped a pair of handcuffs onto the stretcher's arm rail.

"He's not going anywhere," Nicole muttered, yanking the orange safety strap snugly across his chest.

With the help of the officers, they wheeled the stretcher toward the exit.

"I'll be riding with you," one officer said, gripping the stretcher rail and pushing alongside them.

"Maggie, I'll ride in the back with him. Can you grab the clipboard while we load up?" Nicole glanced at her partner, her tone matter-of-fact but protective. Nicole usually drove, but she wanted to stay close in case the man became violent again—she wasn't willing to risk Maggie getting hurt.

"Sure, I'll be right there." Maggie gave a nod, then turned back into the store to make sure they hadn't left any equipment behind.

As she checked the area, Maggie noticed the young employee still standing behind the counter, her hands trembling as she gave her statement to a police officer.

"Are you all right? Do you need to go to the hospital?" Maggie asked gently, stepping closer.

The woman shook her head. "No, I'm not hurt. My boss is coming in. I just... I just need to go home. Thanks for asking."

Maggie picked up the clipboard and stepped out of the building. The stretcher was already loaded, and the ambulance doors were shut. As she reached for the driver's side handle, a sudden jolt to her arm startled her.

She turned quickly—Gary stood beside her, gripping her arm.

"Hey, *Butterfly*. Where's my sister?" he asked.

Maggie flinched. Gary looked terrible—unshaven, strung out. His skin was pale, his eyes sunken and restless. For a moment, she didn't recognize him.

She yanked her arm back. "You scared the crap out of me. What did you just call me?"

Gary pointed at her hair clip—a butterfly with vibrant colors. It was an anniversary gift from Victor's uncle, something she always wore to keep her bangs out of her eyes. Instinctively, Maggie reached up to touch it.

Gary grabbed her arm again, more forcefully this time. "I need to talk to Nicole," he said, spitting his words in a rush.

Maggie twisted free. "Back off, Gary. We're working."

She tried to open the ambulance door, but he held it shut.

"Just tell her I need to talk to her, okay?" he said, his voice low, almost threatening. Then he released the door. "And don't fuck with me."

Maggie climbed into the driver's seat and slammed the door. As she backed out of the parking space, she kept her eyes on Gary. He pulled his collar up, shoved his hands into his coat pockets, and slinked across the street.

She flipped on the sirens and headed for University Hospital, trying to calm her racing heart. She took deep breaths, but it wasn't working.

Gary's appearance had shaken her. But it was that word—*Butterfly*—that really rattled her.

Patricia Castle.

The woman whose husband was murdered in the alley had told Detective Mallory the attacker had called her *Butterfly*, too.

Maggie's stomach tightened.

She started connecting the dots. The fight with the prostitute. The erratic behavior. The things Nicole had confided about her brother. And now this.

The ambulance pulled up in front of the emergency room's sliding doors. Maggie shut off the engine and jumped out. As she rounded the back, she heard shouting from inside. She flung open the rear doors to find the police officer leaning over the stretcher, using his weight to restrain the patient. Nicole was finishing up an IV, her movements calm but quick.

Together, they rolled the stretcher into the ER where a nurse and a doctor were waiting. They gave their report as they transferred the man from the stretcher to the hospital bed. An officer cuffed him to the bed rail just in time—he began to stir, shouting obscenities as his sedation wore off.

Maggie and Nicole didn't wait around.

By the time they'd finished their paperwork and cleaned out the ambulance, things had calmed down. Maggie used the quiet moment to finally say what had been bothering her.

"Gary showed up as I was leaving the store," she said. "He asked me to tell you to call him."

Nicole froze mid-step. "What? Why didn't you tell me sooner?"

"We were kind of busy," Maggie said. "But... there's more. I think I saw him in my backyard the other night."

Nicole's eyes narrowed. "You're kidding. What happened?"

"I don't even know if it was him," Maggie admitted. "It was dark, fast—maybe I was dreaming. I don't know. But still... what's going on with him?"

"I don't know," Nicole muttered. "But I don't like him showing up at your house."

"I don't either." Maggie hesitated, her voice softening. "Nicole... I'm worried. I think Gary might be getting into serious trouble. And I'm scared he might hurt you."

She reached out and took Nicole's hand.

Nicole quickly pulled away, unsettled by the intimacy of the gesture. "He wouldn't hurt me. But he sure as hell shouldn't be anywhere near your place. He has no reason to be on that side of town."

"I honestly can't say for sure it was him," Maggie offered. "So don't worry too much."

"No, I *am* going to worry. And I'm going to find out if it was him," Nicole said. She started to say something else, then stopped herself. Her jaw clenched.

After a pause, Maggie reached over and gave her shoulder a gentle pat. "Come on. Let's go home. Shift's over."

They returned to the station and dropped off the ambulance. Maggie gave Nicole a small wave as she pulled out of the parking lot, heading home. Nicole remained in her car, hesitating. A queasy feeling twisted in her stomach at the thought of Gary prowling around Maggie's house.

After a moment, she started the engine and followed Maggie's route, stopping two houses down from her friend's place. She killed the engine and headlights, cloaking herself in shadow.

From her vantage point, Nicole could see the garage door had closed, and the warm glow of lights lit up Maggie's living room. She had given her friend plenty of time to get home. She wasn't sure exactly why she'd followed—maybe it was the gnawing thought that she'd catch Gary lurking nearby.

Sitting alone in the darkness, her thoughts spiraled. She kept telling herself that whatever people thought about Gary, they didn't know him. Yes, he had a rough past, a screwed-up childhood—but he wasn't a killer. He wasn't evil.

An hour passed. No sign of Gary. No movement, no disturbance. Nicole was just beginning to feel reassured when a red truck turned into Maggie's driveway. Her hand froze on the ignition.

The garage door opened slowly, and the truck pulled in beside Maggie's BMW. Victor stepped out, wiping his hands on a cloth. He walked to the front of the house and paused. Looking both ways down the street, his gaze fixed on something in the distance.

Nicole followed his line of sight. A hooded figure stood at the far end of the block, just beyond the reach of the streetlight.

Her heart thudded. She watched Victor and the figure in tense silence. Neither moved. Then Victor turned back, pressed the garage remote, and disappeared inside as the door closed behind him.

Nicole's eyes darted back to the spot where the hooded man had been—but he was gone.

Gone.

Her pulse quickened. She waited a moment longer to be sure Victor had gone inside, then started her engine and slowly rolled past Maggie's house, scanning the shadows.

No sign of him.

Whoever it was had vanished into the night.

She found herself doubting what she saw. The man had seemed broader, taller than Gary—but she couldn't be sure. And Victor... Had he been watching for Gary? He didn't look alarmed. More like he was expecting someone.

Wild scenarios ran through her mind. None of them made sense.

When Nicole finally pulled up in front of her own house, a wave of relief washed over her. At least she didn't have work tomorrow.

CHAPTER EIGHTEEN

The wind tossed the bare branches back and forth with vigorous force. Tall trees, stark and leafless like skeletal sentinels, crowded this part of the woods. A narrow dirt path veered off from the road and wound its way into the dense grove.

Hidden within the thicket was a small stream, about ten feet wide, snaking through the quiet land. Its water was clear and shallow, revealing smooth stones, jagged rocks, and bits of trash caught in the slow current. Overhead, the sun lay cloaked behind thick clouds, casting a hazy light across the cool mid-afternoon air.

Half-concealed among the trees, a boy pressed his body against the trunk of an old oak. His blonde hair tousled in the wind, and his cheeks were flushed pink from the chill. He wore a shabby jacket with missing buttons, a faded scarf knotted around his neck, and a pair of mismatched gloves that barely covered his fingers. He leaned into the tree, watching the path with sharp attention.

His eyes lit up when he spotted movement—a little girl approaching from the road, walking toward the stream. She wore an old blue jacket with a black velvet collar, its front pocket pinned shut to hold it in place. Her long blonde hair was pulled back into a ponytail. Slung across her shoulder was a pink school bag, and in her hand, she carried a small lunchbox. Like the boy, her cheeks were red from the cold, and a trace of nasal drip glistened under her nose, a detail of the damp weather.

As she drew closer, passing the very tree the boy hid behind, he grew visibly tense—like a cat poised to pounce. Then, suddenly, he lunged from his hiding place, landing directly in her path.

Startled, the girl cried out and dropped her lunchbox with a clatter. The boy grabbed her arms, laughing as he began to paw at her, his touch more mischievous than harmful.

The little girl shoved the boy away and quickly stooped to retrieve her lunchbox. Without saying a word, she stepped back onto the path, which cut across the shallow stream via a narrow wooden bridge and continued on the other side.

The boy followed her, walking along the streambank. When he caught up, he grabbed her from behind, clumsily trying to hold her. Then, with a sudden burst of force, he knocked her to the ground.

The girl lay stunned in the dirt, and the boy stood over her, breathing hard. He unzipped his trousers. As she tried to sit up, he pushed her back down, continuing to pull down his underwear and shoved his privates against her face.

No," she whimpered, turning her head and trying to crawl away. Tears streaked her cheeks.

The boy grabbed the back of her head and forced himself toward her again, now rougher, seemingly unaware of her growing distress.

She flailed, smacking at him blindly. One of her hands struck him low in the stomach, causing him to grunt in pain. Reflexively, perhaps out of confusion or frustration, he lashed out, his fist catching her cheek.

The girl crumpled sideways with a soft gasp, her head striking a jagged rock half-buried in the soil. The boy froze.

He stood there, eyes wide, breathing heavily. The boy masturbated, standing over the girl, only taking a few minutes to ejaculate. Then he dropped to his knees beside her and shook her gently. "Emma?" he whispered. "Get up."

She didn't move.

He rolled her onto her back. Her eyes were open but vacant, staring at the gray sky. Just then, a thin stream of blood ran from her nose and across her temple.

****

"No!" Victor jolted upright in bed, his body drenched in sweat, breath ragged and shallow.

Maggie stirred beside him, startled from sleep. "What is it?" she asked, blinking in the darkness. "What's wrong?"

Victor didn't respond right away. He sat motionless, trying to slow his breathing.

Maggie reached out, placing a gentle hand on his damp back as she propped herself up on one elbow. "Victor, are you okay? You're sweating... Are you sick?"

"I'm all right," he said hoarsely. "Just a bad dream. Go back to sleep." He wiped his face with the edge of the sheet.

Maggie turned to glance at the clock on the nightstand. The red digits read 3:00 AM.

"I didn't hear you come in," she murmured. "I must've passed out the second my head hit the pillow. What time did you get home?"

"Around midnight," Victor replied. "Had some paperwork to finish. Go back to sleep."

He lay back down, draping his forearm across his forehead. Maggie turned onto her side, nestling close to him and resting her head on his shoulder.

She tried to settle back into sleep, but her mind wouldn't quiet. The jolt of being woken lingered, and she couldn't stop thinking about Gary—something just didn't feel right.

Meanwhile, Victor's thoughts spiraled elsewhere—back to the dream, back to the moment that haunted him: his sister's lifeless eyes staring up at the sky.

Later that morning, Maggie was stirred awake by the sharp ring of the phone. She blinked and reached for the cordless handset, noticing Victor's side of the bed was already empty.

"Hello?" she croaked, her voice still thick with sleep.

"Hey, Maggie—did I wake you?" Nicole's voice chimed through the line.

Maggie shielded her eyes from the sunlight creeping through the curtains. "No, it's fine. What time is it?"

"Almost eleven. Get up, sleepyhead! I need to run to the mall and was wondering if you wanted to hang out for a bit."

"Hmm... yeah, I guess. Do you want me to meet you there?"

"Yep, in front of that giant boot sculpture. I'll be waiting at the coffee shop."

Maggie was more awake now. "All right. Give me an hour. Bye."

She hung up and lay back for a moment, letting her thoughts drift. Her mind returned to Victor's nightmare from the night before. Something about it unsettled her deeply. There was more going on—she could feel it.

Dragging herself out of bed, she got dressed, deciding this might be a good time to talk to Nicole. Maybe she could help make sense of the uneasy feeling that had settled over her thoughts about Gary.

An hour later, Nicole sat on a bench bolted to the ground outside her favorite coffee shop. She wore blue jeans and a faded blue T-shirt, sipping from a to-go cup as she waited.

When she spotted Maggie approaching, she smiled and stood up.

Were you waiting long?" Maggie asked, reaching to hug her.

Nicole returned the hug a little hesitantly. Affection always made her nervous around Maggie. She worried that her feelings might show more than she intended.

No, I just got here." Nicole handed her a second cup. I got you a coffee. I m glad you came. I just... didn t feel like being alone today."

Yeah, I m glad you called," Maggie said with a smile. Otherwise, I probably would ve stayed in bed all day."

She looped her arm through Nicole s, gently guiding her to walk. They spent the next couple of hours meandering through the mall, ducking in and out of shops. By the time they headed toward the parking garage, their hands were full of department store bags, and their conversation had become light and easy.

Just as they passed a water fountain, a voice called out from a few feet away.

Maggie? Is that you?"

A woman in her late forties with reddish-dyed hair waved enthusiastically. Maggie turned, startled. Yes?" she answered, uncertain.

The woman's face lit up. "You don't recognize me, do you? That's all right, honey. I know Victor. I only met you once, a long time ago." Her words came fast, her hands gesturing wildly as she spoke.

Before Maggie could say anything, the woman pressed on. "My husband worked with Victor up north. You're much prettier than his last wife. Honestly, it was the best thing that ever happened when she ran off and left him."

Maggie blinked, thrown off. "I'm sorry... what did you say? Victor's ex-wife died."

She glanced at Nicole, who looked equally confused.

"No, no, no," the woman said, waving a hand. "That tramp left him. Just like that—poof! Gone. That's why Victor moved away. Poor guy just couldn't take the heartbreak. I can't believe I recognized you! You haven't changed a bit. Don't you remember? We met at his office Christmas party. No worries, I forget people all the time."

Maggie opened her mouth to respond, but the woman barreled on without pause.

"Listen, sweetie, I have to go. It's nice to see you—you look great. Keep doing whatever you're doing, honey. Bye now!"

The woman turned and walked off just as quickly as she'd appeared, vanishing into the crowd.

Maggie stood frozen for a moment, then turned to Nicole, her face still registering shock. "Wow... what was that all about?"

Nicole shrugged. "Maybe she confused you with someone else."

"I don't know. She knew Victor's name... and I have been to his firm's Christmas party. She seemed so sure she recognized me. That was just... weird." Maggie shook her head, watching the woman disappear into the bustling mall.

Nicole began walking toward the parking garage but paused as she spotted a large flat-screen TV in a store window playing the news. Wait—hang on a sec. I want to see this."

She stepped into the store entrance, eyes fixed on the screen. Maggie followed and stood beside her.

The news anchor was reporting a murder that had taken place downtown the previous night. Detective Mallory appeared on-screen, giving a brief statement to the press.

Maggie stiffened. Her thoughts instantly jumped to Gary.

Nicole... do you think Gary—?"

No," Nicole interrupted firmly, already turning away. Not possible."

Maggie lingered in front of the screen, still unsettled. A few feet ahead, Nicole called over her shoulder, Are you coming?"

Maggie sighed, exasperated, and followed. All right," she said quietly, I won t bring it up again."

Thank you."

Later that afternoon, Maggie tried calling Victor while driving home from the mall. The call went straight to voicemail—his assistant said he was in a meeting.

Her mind kept replaying the mall encounter. *Victor s ex-wife didn t die? She just... left him? Why would he lie?*

The unease stayed with her until Victor came home around five. She heard the garage door hum open and close. That familiar sound filled her with a strange mix of relief and anxiety.

She was glad to see him—glad, in fact, that they could spend the evening together—but a chill of hesitation stirred inside her. Victor's recent moods had become more unpredictable. Small things seemed to set him off, and Maggie found herself growing more cautious around him.

She stood at the stove, stirring a pot of sauce, her heart ticking louder with every approaching footstep. Part of her wanted to confront him right away about the woman at the mall—but another part feared the reaction it might provoke.

Not tonight, she decided. Not yet.

CHAPTER NINETEEN

An orange ball of fire peeked over the horizon, casting warm hues into the fading shades of blue. On the opposite end of the sky, the last pale glow of the moon clung to the darkness, dissolving as morning claimed the day.

Nicole sat in her SUV, parked in Maggie's driveway. She gave a short honk of the horn and glanced toward the house. Through the window, she saw Maggie wave—a quick signal that she knew Nicole was waiting.

Moments later, the front door swung open. Maggie stepped out, coffee mug in hand, and slid into the passenger seat with a groggy huff.

"So," she said, setting her drink into the cup holder, "what do you know so far?"

Nicole pulled the car into drive. "Jeff said they still haven't found her. She's been missing for about fourteen hours. Her parents said they just looked away for a minute, and she was gone."

Maggie pulled her hair back into a ponytail, trying to wake herself up. "Since last night? God... that's terrifying."

Nicole nodded, eyes on the road. "Yeah. She's either really scared… or someone took her." She glanced at Maggie, then smirked. "You look like hell this morning. Didn't sleep?"

"Thanks. You look great, too," Maggie shot back dryly, then gave Nicole a light punch on the arm. "No, not really. I've been tense lately. I still haven't asked Victor about his ex-wife. He's been so moody. I mean, maybe that woman at the mall was wrong, but it's still bugging me."

Nicole glanced sideways again. "You two still having problems?"

"I guess it's more *my* problem. He doesn't seem to think it's an issue. But he's been snapping more lately—those bursts of anger… I don't know. Men are so damn complicated." As the SUV bounced over a pothole, Maggie spilled a bit of coffee on her shirt. "Ugh."

"What, are you trying to bathe in it?" Nicole teased, chuckling. "And for the record, women are just as complicated. That's why I'm still single."

"Oh? And here I thought you were just waiting for me." Maggie grinned, her tone teasing, eyes glinting.

Nicole was caught off guard. Her breath hitched slightly, and she blushed, turning her focus back to the road.

Maggie noticed immediately. "Hey, I'm sorry. Just messing with you, dork."

Nicole tried to brush it off with a smile. "Yeah, whatever."

But the warmth lingered on her cheeks, and the truth lingered too. What Maggie had said was half a joke, maybe even a quarter joke. Still… there was truth in it. A truth Nicole would never admit—not out loud.

Nicole had received a phone call from Jeff Peterson, the chief of the fire station in Fredericksburg. A seven-year-old girl had gone missing the previous evening in Enchanted Rock Park, a rugged area just outside the small German town known for its bed and breakfasts and antique shops. Fredericksburg, a quiet and quaint tourist destination, is located about an hour and a half north of San Antonio.

As a volunteer with the fire station, Nicole had been called to assist in the search and rescue mission. The girl had disappeared somewhere within the park s vast wilderness reserve, which sprawled across the Texas landscape and featured hiking and biking trails, along with campsites available for rent.

According to initial reports, a young couple had been enjoying a picnic with family and friends when they noticed their daughter was missing. The picnic site had been set up far from the parking area, near the tree line, leading them to believe she may have wandered into the woods.

When Nicole arrived at the park s lot, the morning sun had already climbed high, its rays casting heat waves off the black asphalt. A large tent had been set up to serve as the command post for the rescue operation. She parked and checked in.

Jeff greeted her, a headset in one ear and a walkie-talkie in his hand. Hey, Nicole, thanks for coming."

Jeff, this is Maggie, my partner... my EMS partner," she added quickly, flustered. Then, trying to recover, she asked, Have you found her yet?"

No, I m afraid not. Let me show you what we re dealing with."

He led them to a board displaying a map of the park grounds. I have teams in both these areas," he said, pointing. I d like you to start here and work your way north. You should meet up with one of the other teams near this rock formation." Jeff traced a path across the map with his finger as he spoke.

How can I reach you, and what's the girl's name?" Nicole asked as Maggie glanced around at the people gathered nearby. Off to the side, she noticed a woman, likely in her mid-twenties, crying, her head buried in her hands, a handkerchief clenched tightly in one fist. A distraught young man paced anxiously in front of her.

Her name is Bianca. She's seven." Jeff handed Nicole a two-way radio. Here, take this—and make sure you've got enough water. We don't need any of the volunteers getting dehydrated."

Testing, one, two, three," Nicole said, pressing the button to check if the radio worked properly.

Jeff smiled, ignoring the chatter that crackled through his own radio.

Let's go," Nicole said to Maggie as they grabbed their backpacks, which were stocked with water, nutrition bars, and basic first-aid supplies.

They started down one of the trails Jeff had shown them on the map. The path was narrow and well-trodden—a clear sign from the trampled earth that it saw regular use. Grass no longer grew there. Because of its width, they had to walk in a single line. Nicole led the way, dressed in khaki shorts and a short-sleeved blue denim shirt. She wore brown hiking boots and white socks that rose just above her ankles. Her legs were muscular, smooth, and freshly shaven.

Maggie, trailing behind, couldn't help but notice Nicole's fit body—after all, it had been her main view for the past hour. She admired Nicole's figure, secretly thinking it was perfect, even though Nicole herself was far from confident in her appearance. Nicole was, as always, her own worst critic.

Maggie, meanwhile, regretted her footwear choice. She had opted for hiking boots instead of her usual tennis shoes, and they hadn't been broken in properly. A blister was already forming on her heel, and they hadn't even been walking that long.

"Hey, let's rest for a minute—my feet are killing me," Maggie said, stopping to sit on a nearby tree stump. She unlaced one of her boots and exposed her foot, inspecting the blister that had begun to form.

"Ouch. That looks like it hurts," Nicole said, reaching into her backpack and pulling out a bottle of water. After taking a sip, she held it out to Maggie. "Do you want a drink?"

"No thanks, I brought some too." Maggie pulled a 24-oz. bottle from her own bag. After re-lacing her boot, she splashed a bit of water on her neck, letting the cool droplets ease the heat radiating from her skin. Behind her sunglasses, Nicole watched silently as Maggie enjoyed the brief relief.

"Come on, let's keep going," Nicole said, snapping herself out of her thoughts as they resumed the search.

They made their way back down the narrow trail and soon reached the base of one of the large rock formations. Nicole pulled out a compass and held it up, watching the needle settle.

"Do you actually know how to use that, or is it just for looks?" Maggie teased, smiling.

"Yes, I took a survival class one summer. I know how to use a compass, smart-ass," Nicole muttered with a smirk. "Let's go up the rock here and see what's on the other side." She pointed ahead, motioning for Maggie to take the lead.

"Sure, now you want me in front. So if I fall, you'll know not to go that way," Maggie joked as she took a big stride up the rock.

It's in case you fall—I can catch you," Nicole replied, smiling as she followed.

At the top, they had to navigate carefully around a scatter of rocks to reach the other side. As they moved forward, Maggie paused, her head tilting slightly.

Stop! Do you hear that?" she said sharply.

Both women stood still, listening. Nicole, slightly winded from the climb, held her breath. Then it came again, a faint, distant cry.

Another, slightly louder cry followed. Without hesitation, they began moving faster in the direction of the sound, adrenaline overriding fatigue.

They called out as they hurried along the rocky terrain. Bianca, we hear you! Keep calling out to us!" Nicole shouted. Can you hear me? We're coming, Bianca! Hold on!" Maggie echoed, both their voices filled with urgency and hope.

As they reached the side of one of the rocks, Maggie slipped, losing her footing. Nicole reacted quickly, grabbing her arm and preventing her from falling into a small crevice between two rocks.

Be careful. I got you," Nicole said, helping Maggie regain her balance.

Both women stood still, peering down into the narrow gap. Inside, they saw a small girl with reddish-brown hair and dirt on her tear-streaked face, looking up at them and crying.

Bianca, it's okay. We're here to help you," Maggie said gently, crouching beside the opening. Your name is Bianca, right... honey?"

The little girl sniffled and replied shyly, I fell down. I want my mommy," before bursting into tears again.

"It's all right, sweetheart. We're going to take you to your mommy," Maggie reassured her. "Are you hurt anywhere, Bianca?"

"No, I don't think so. I'm hungry… I want my mommy."

Nicole pulled out the two-way radio and contacted Jeff. "We found her," she said. "We're near the north side of the rock formation—close to marker six. She's okay, just shaken up."

Meanwhile, Maggie laid flat on her stomach, reaching both arms into the crevice.

"Come on, sweetie. Reach your arms up to me," she coaxed softly.

Bianca stretched her little arms upward. Nicole bent down to assist, and together, they carefully pulled the girl out of the hole. Once free, Nicole scooped her up, holding her securely in her arms. Bianca immediately wrapped her arms and legs around her, clinging tightly.

"It's all right. You're safe now—it's okay," Nicole whispered, cradling her. "How did you manage to get up here?"

"I was chasing a butterfly," Bianca said, her voice muffled against Nicole's shoulder. "Then I got lost. I thought if I got on top of the rock, I could see my mommy and daddy. I was scared… it was dark and cold."

Nicole held her close, brushing dirt gently from the girl's hair. "It's all right. Your daddy's on his way—he's coming on a motorbike, and you'll get to ride back with him. Here, have a little water."

Maggie opened a bottle and held it to Bianca's lips, letting her take small sips. As the girl drank, Maggie gently ran her hands over her back and legs, checking for any injuries.

In the distance, the muffled sounds of four-wheelers grew louder.

Working together, Maggie and Nicole carefully made their way down from the rock, Nicole still holding the girl tightly in her arms.

Four all-terrain vehicles arrived, kicking up dust as they came to a stop. Bianca's father rode as a passenger on the second one. The comfort of Nicole's arms was instantly forgotten when the little girl spotted him. She nearly toppled out of Nicole's embrace as she leapt down and ran to her father, who scooped her up and held her tightly, kissing her tear-streaked cheek.

Jeff was among the men who had arrived. He walked over to Nicole, a relieved smile on his face.

"Nice work. She's lucky—there are coyotes out here at night."

"Actually," Nicole said, brushing dirt from her shorts, "she fell into a hole up there. It probably kept her safe. Better there than wandering in the woods."

"Come on—we'll give you both a ride back." Jeff placed a friendly hand on Nicole's shoulder and gestured toward the four-wheelers.

Each vehicle had room for two riders. Nicole climbed onto one with Jeff, while Maggie rode with one of the other rescuers.

Back at the command station, the scene had already begun winding down. Volunteers were packing up gear, and the tent was being dismantled. Bianca's mother—still teary-eyed—rushed forward as the vehicles pulled in. Nicole watched quietly as the family reunited, feeling a deep, satisfying peace knowing she had played a part in something meaningful.

The drive back to San Antonio was quiet. Nicole and Maggie listened to music, the silence between them comfortable. They made a quick stop at a fast food restaurant, sharing fries and sipping sodas. The return trip somehow felt shorter, as if the weight of the day had shifted.

When Nicole pulled into Maggie's driveway, she glanced over. "Do you want to come in?" she asked.

Maggie shook her head. No, I better get home. I want a shower and a nap—I m exhausted. Thanks for everything today."

Thanks for coming along. I really think you should sign up to volunteer. You were great out there," Nicole said.

Maggie smiled, waving as she rummaged through her purse for her keys.

Nicole waited until Maggie disappeared inside, then pulled out of the driveway and headed home. The afternoon sun still hung high in the sky, casting long rays across the pavement. Drained from the early start and the long hours in the heat, Nicole let out a deep sigh of relief, knowing she would soon be home and able to go to sleep.

CHAPTER TWENTY

Raindrops beat rhythmically against the windshield, the wipers slicing through the downpour in a tireless, mechanical arc. Daylight had all but vanished, swallowed by the hazy gray of early evening. The sky rumbled with distant thunder, and flashes of lightning revealed thick storm clouds looming overhead. It felt eerily familiar.

Maggie and Nicole maneuvered their ambulance into the narrow alleyway behind a row of buildings near the Alamodome. Another rape call. Another alley. Another night where the world felt indifferent.

Police cruisers lined the street, their red and blue lights reflecting off wet pavement. Officers moved with purpose, yellow tape marking off the area. At the far end of the alley, near a dumpster behind a restaurant, Detective Mallory crouched beside a woman wrapped in a blanket, her back pressed to a cold, damp brick wall.

Maggie and Nicole stepped out, their boots splashing in puddles as they pulled the stretcher and equipment toward the victim. Mallory looked up as they approached, standing and brushing rain from his notebook.

"This is Kim Smith," he said, squinting at Maggie's badge. "Mrs. Reed. She was attacked here, beaten badly. A storeowner found her and called it in."

Kim's face told the rest of the story. One eye was swollen shut, her mouth split and bleeding. Her hands trembled beneath the blanket. Rainwater ran down her cheek, mixing with the blood.

Maggie knelt beside her, speaking softly. Nicole began unpacking supplies.

Mallory stepped back, continuing to jot down notes.

"Do you have any questions for me?" he asked, barely glancing up. "Otherwise, I need to move on."

Maggie looked up. "Ah... no, we've got it. You're not riding with us?"

"I've already questioned her. I've got follow-ups to handle. I'll have an officer trail you to the hospital for evidence collection." He turned, already focused on his notebook again.

As he walked away, Maggie shared a quiet look with Nicole—professional, steady, but heavy. Another long night had begun.

Maggie and Nicole worked swiftly and quietly, a practiced rhythm between them as they stabilized Kim on the stretcher. They cleaned the worst of the blood from her face, applied gauze to slow the bleeding, then gently secured her to the stretcher before loading her into the back of the ambulance. Nicole climbed in beside her.

Before Maggie closed the rear doors, she tore a sheet of paper from her chart, scribbled her name and phone number, then folded it. With a quick glance at Nicole to make sure everything was under control, she jogged across the slick alley to where Detective Mallory stood beneath a dripping awning, still flipping through his notes.

"Excuse me," she said, holding out the folded paper.

Mallory looked up, brow furrowing.

I can't talk now," Maggie continued. "But do you think you could call me tomorrow? I think I might have some information... something I need to talk to you about."

Mallory straightened slightly, his attention sharpening. "If you know something, don't wait until tomorrow."

Maggie hesitated, hugging her arms against the chill. "I don't know if it's anything yet. I just—please. Call me tomorrow. I'll explain everything then."

He studied her for a moment, then nodded. "Alright, Mrs. Reed. I'll call you in the morning."

Maggie turned without another word and ran back to the ambulance, slamming the doors shut. She climbed into the driver's seat and pulled away from the alley, headed toward the hospital through the slick, puddled streets.

After dropping Kim off and handing her off to the ER staff, Maggie and Nicole made their way to the roof of University Hospital—a quiet place to decompress before heading home. They sat in silence for a while, watching the rain clouds break apart as early dawn crept over the city.

The next morning, Maggie stirred awake to the sound of the shower running. Victor was up. She had slept fitfully, her mind knotted with the memory of Kim's face, and the gnawing suspicion she hadn't yet named.

Slipping out of bed, she padded downstairs. The air was still cool with the last of the night's rain. She switched on the coffee maker and opened the back door for Wrangler, who trotted outside with his tail high, sniffing the ground as if each blade of grass held a secret.

Maggie stood at the doorway, a fresh cup of coffee warming her hands. The morning light was crisp and gold, the sky scrubbed clean from the storm. She took a slow breath, trying to let it clear her thoughts. But the unease lingered.

Victor entered the kitchen, his dress shirt tucked in, tie slung around his neck, still loose. He glanced at her as he reached for his travel mug.

"You're up early," he said.

"Yeah," Maggie murmured, not looking away from the yard. "Didn't sleep much."

Victor gave her a curious look but didn't press. "Long night?"

She nodded.

Maggie stayed where she was, sipping coffee, eyes following Wrangler as he darted around the wet grass.

She didn't hear the phone ring, but she knew—Mallory would call.

"I wondered where you were. I saw your side of the bed was empty," Victor said, stepping into the kitchen.

"I couldn't sleep," Maggie replied with a yawn.

"I hope I didn't wake you?"

"No, I just have a lot on my mind." She moved to pour him a cup of coffee, her movements slow and deliberate. "Hey, you were only married once before, right?" she asked, handing him the mug.

Victor took it, his brow tightening as he studied her. "Yeah... why?"

"I thought so. No reason."

He tilted his head slightly. "Is everything alright?"

"Yes. It's nothing," she said with a quick smile, one that didn't quite reach her eyes. She turned away before he could study her more closely.

Victor picked up his briefcase and headed toward the garage. As he reached to open the door, a man was already walking up the driveway. Tall, trench coat still damp from morning dew—Detective Mallory.

"Good morning. Are you Mr. Reed?"

Victor paused, his instincts on edge. "Yes. Can I help you?"

"I'm Detective Mallory with the Police Department." He extended a hand. "I was hoping to speak with your wife, Maggie. We met last night at a crime scene. She asked me to stop by."

Victor shook his hand, still guarded. "Is something wrong?"

"No, not at all. She just said she had something she wanted to discuss. I hope I'm not intruding."

Before Victor could respond, the door to the house opened. Maggie stepped out into the garage.

"I thought I heard voices. Hello, Detective Mallory." She smiled. "How did you know where I live?" Then, catching herself, "Oh—never mind. You're a cop. Of course, you know how to find people."

Mallory gave a polite nod. "Good morning, Mrs. Reed."

"Would you like to come in for some coffee?"

"Sure. That sounds great."

Victor opened his truck door and placed his briefcase inside. Maggie noticed he hadn't left yet.

"You don't have to stay," she said gently. "I just want to talk with Detective Mallory for a bit. In private."

Victor hesitated, clearly uncomfortable. "Are you sure? I don't mind sticking around."

"No, please. Don't let me keep you from work."

He nodded slowly. "Call me later, alright?" His voice carried a faint note of concern.

"I will."

With one last glance between them, Victor got into his truck and pulled out of the driveway. Maggie watched until he turned the corner, then motioned for Mallory to follow her inside.

Maggie and Detective Mallory stepped inside, the warmth of the house a stark contrast to the tension in her chest. She poured him a cup of coffee, and they sat in the quiet of the living room.

For nearly an hour, Maggie spoke. She told him about Gary—Nicole's brother—and her uneasy suspicions. The detective listened intently, jotting notes in his pad, his expression unreadable but focused.

"I know it's just a feeling," Maggie said, "but I can't shake it. Something about Gary... he gives me the creeps. Always has."

Mallory nodded, his pen still moving. "Instincts are worth listening to, especially when they come from someone like you who's been in the field."

Before he left, Mallory's eyes wandered around the room. A habit, perhaps, but one that never turned off. His gaze paused on a framed photo on the mantel.

"Somewhere in the Caribbean?" he asked, gesturing.

"Grand Cayman," Maggie said, following his eyes. "Victor and I went scuba diving there last month."

She noticed the way he scanned the room, assessing, like he was still forming a profile of her. Maggie wondered if he thought she was just a stressed-out medic cracking under pressure. Maybe she was.

When he left, the house fell silent. She tried to go back to bed, but rest wouldn't come. Guilt tugged at her chest. Was she betraying Nicole? Was she paranoid?

Her alarm blared, reminding her that duty still called.

As she reached to shut it off, Victor walked into the bedroom, startling her.

"What are you doing home?" she asked through a yawn. "I wasn't expecting you."

"I just... didn't like leaving with that detective here this morning." He sat on the edge of the bed, his face drawn with concern. "Is everything alright? What's going on?"

Maggie hesitated, then sighed. "It's about Nicole's brother. Gary. I told Detective Mallory I think he might be connected to the recent rapes."

Victor's brow furrowed. "Nicole? Your partner?"

"Yeah. Gary's... trouble. Always has been. He gives off this energy that's just... off. I didn't want to believe it at first, but the more I think about it, the more it adds up."

"So that's all the detective wanted to talk about?"

"I asked him to come," she admitted. "I needed to tell someone who could actually do something. But now, I feel like I'm betraying Nicole. I haven't told her any of this."

Victor was quiet for a moment.

And... there's something else," Maggie added. "I didn't tell you before, but a few nights ago—when you were already asleep—I thought I saw someone in the backyard. A man. I'm not sure, but... it could've been Gary."

Victor stiffened. "What? Why didn't you tell me?"

"I didn't want to worry you. It was dark, raining—I told myself I imagined it. But now..." She trailed off, pressing her hand to her forehead. "I don't know what to think."

She looked up at him, her eyes tired but grateful. "Thanks. I just hope I'm not making a mistake."

"Why didn't you tell me... what did he look like?" Victor's tone sharpened, his concern now edged with alarm.

"I couldn't really see his face," Maggie said softly. "He was wearing one of those zip-up hooded jackets. I—I don't know why I didn't say anything sooner. I'm sorry."

Victor's expression darkened. He leaned back, his mind drifting. "Three times," he murmured.

"What?"

"I've seen a guy with a hooded jacket watching me. Once outside the gym. Another time when I picked you up from work. And... one night, right out front."

Maggie sat up straighter, wrapping her arms around his neck. "Are you okay?"

He kissed her temple but didn't answer right away. "Yeah. I need to get back to work," he finally said. "Just wanted to check on you."

She could tell—his body was here, but his thoughts were still chasing shadows.

After walking Wrangler, Maggie got ready and headed to the station. The drive felt unusually long, her thoughts a blur of fear and doubt. Had she stirred something that should've been left alone?

She pulled her black BMW into the gated staff lot and turned off the ignition. Reaching across the seat for her purse and notebook, a sudden *thud* slammed into the driver's side window. She jolted, heart leaping into her throat.

Gary.

His fist struck the glass again. And again.

Maggie's breath caught. She didn't dare open the door. With shaking hands, she cracked the window just an inch.

"You listen to me, bitch," Gary growled, his face twisted with rage. "Your little detective friend's been sniffin' around. You better keep your mouth shut. You hear me? Crazy bitch."

He spat at the window. The saliva smeared down the glass as his hand slapped it one more time before he stormed off.

Maggie sat frozen, her body tense as a bowstring, eyes wide, breath shallow. The world outside muffled as her heartbeat pounded in her ears.

Then she saw Nicole's car pull into the lot. Nicole stepped out just in time to catch Gary turning the corner, disappearing down the street. She walked over quickly, noticing the open crack in Maggie's window and her pale, stricken face.

"Maggie? What the hell just happened?" Nicole asked, alarmed.

Maggie tried to speak, but nothing came out.

Nicole's eyes narrowed. "Was that... my brother?"

Here's

"Hey, what's up? Was that Gary?" Nicole asked, her voice already tense.

Maggie nodded as she stepped out of the car, her nerves still buzzing. Yeah. He called me a bitch and told me to mind my own business."

What? Why is he bothering you?" Nicole's eyes flared with immediate concern.

I don't know," Maggie said, hesitating. She wanted to tell Nicole about her conversation with Detective Mallory, but something held her back. Maybe fear. Maybe guilt.

Nicole clenched her fists. I need to find him and put a stop to this. I *don't* think he's the one behind the rapes, but he *is* out of control, and he can't go around harassing you like this."

Please, just let it go," Maggie said, placing a hand on Nicole's arm. He's upset. I don't want you running around downtown looking for him, not with everything else going on. If he contacts me again, I'll tell you. I promise."

Nicole looked unconvinced, her face flushed with frustration. I can't make any promises. Maggie, this is getting insane. I'm worried about you... the guy in your yard, Gary acting like this. I don't know what I'd do if something happened to you."

I told you—I'm not even sure what I saw that night. Maybe it wasn't even him."

Nicole nodded slowly, but she wasn't convinced. She remembered the hooded man standing down the street, staring toward Victor's house. What she couldn't admit—what she *didn't* want to admit—was that she had seen it while staking out Maggie's neighborhood herself, too concerned to stay away. Too afraid of what might happen.

Let's just get to work," Nicole said quietly.

Later that evening, the city of San Antonio glowed beneath the shifting hues of twilight. The skyline stood tall and striking, silhouetted against a sky splashed with orange, violet, and indigo. From their parked ambulance, Maggie and Nicole had a perfect view of the Tower of the Americas, framed by the fading sun.

The heat had broken, giving way to a cool, gentle breeze that slipped through the windows. They sat quietly, picking at their takeout. The silence between them wasn t awkward—it was loaded. Heavy with unspoken thoughts.

Hours passed with barely a word, each woman lost in her own spiral of doubt and worry.

Finally, Nicole exhaled hard and broke the silence. All right, I can t take this anymore. I m going downtown to look for Gary. He usually dumpster dives with some of the drunks on Flores Street."

She turned the key and the ambulance rumbled to life.

Nicole..." Maggie started, but the words faded.

Nicole didn t look at her. Her jaw was tight, hands firm on the wheel. I need to make sure he s not spiraling. I just have to."

As the ambulance pulled away from the skyline, the shadows of night crept further across the city, one step closer to whatever truths they were trying to outrun.

Maggie crumpled the empty sandwich bag in her hand and took her final bite. All right," she said through a mouthful. If that ll make you feel better. But I still think we should just leave it alone."

Nicole didn t answer. She was focused, maneuvering the ambulance slowly through the narrow, dim back alleys. She rolled down the window and leaned out, questioning anyone she saw—people sitting against brick walls or rummaging through trash bins.

Some knew Gary by name. Others shook their heads, uninterested or unaware. Maggie sat quietly, arms folded, watching the growing worry on Nicole s face.

The sun had fully vanished now, replaced by a pale half-moon hanging above the city. The shadows deepened, and the alleyways began to feel like tunnels—tight, dark, and endless.

Suddenly, Nicole spotted a figure.

There." She pointed ahead, eyes sharp. I think that was him."

A man in a hooded jacket had just turned the corner at the far end of the alley.

Nicole stopped the ambulance, but the path narrowed—too tight for the vehicle to continue.

I'm going after him," she said, already reaching for the door.

What? No." Maggie sat up straighter, alarmed. You're not going down there."

I'll be right back. Lock the doors," Nicole said over her shoulder, stepping out.

Nicole, this is a bad idea! I *really* wish you'd listen to me!" Maggie called out, but it was too late.

Nicole was already jogging down the alley. She pulled her flashlight from her pocket as the foul scent of rotting food and old urine thickened the air. Her footsteps echoed between the buildings.

Gary?" she called out.

She reached the end of the alley and turned the corner.

This stretch was darker—no streetlights, no car beams. Only the narrow shaft of light from her flashlight guided her way. The darkness pressed close, suffocating and silent.

She took a few cautious steps forward.

Then—without warning—an arm shot out of the darkness and clamped tightly around her neck.

Nicole gasped as she was yanked backward, her flashlight slipping from her hand and clattering to the ground. The man's other hand reached down and grabbed her roughly between her legs. With a terrifying strength, he hoisted her off the ground, pinning her tightly to his chest.

She couldn't scream. Couldn't breathe. The sound of blood pounded in her ears as she kicked and flailed, desperate to break free.

Come here, my little butterfly... I've got something for you," a low, unfamiliar voice whispered in Nicole's ear.

A sick wave of fear shot through her. But instinct and adrenaline took over. With a sharp twist of her body, she drove her elbow into his ribs and kicked back hard with her heel. He grunted in pain and loosened his grip.

Nicole tore free and sprinted back the way she had come, her boots slapping hard against the wet pavement.

Around the corner, Maggie sat rigidly in the front seat of the ambulance, her eyes fixed on the alley. Her heart lurched when she saw Nicole rounding the corner, a dark figure chasing her close behind.

Maggie reacted without thinking—she flipped on the ambulance's headlights and blared the sirens.

The sudden explosion of sound and light stunned the attacker. He hesitated for a heartbeat, then turned and bolted into the shadows.

Nicole yanked open the driver's door and climbed in, gasping for breath.

"Oh my god..." she choked out, her voice shaking as she tried to steady herself.

"What happened? Who was that?" Maggie asked, eyes darting toward the alley, checking for movement.

Nicole wiped her forehead, still panting. "I don't know who he was. He grabbed me, called me 'butterfly.' It wasn't Gary. It was someone else."

"Are you *sure* it wasn't him?" Maggie asked.

"Yes, I'm sure!" Nicole snapped, then caught herself. "Sorry. It wasn't Gary. That guy scared the hell out of me."

"Oh my god," Maggie whispered. "What do we do—should we call the police?"

"I don't know. He's probably long gone by now. I didn't even see his face. But Maggie—"

She paused, glancing at her partner, fear giving way to something heavier. "I think... I think I've seen him before. Outside your house."

Maggie froze. "What are you talking about? When?"

Nicole hesitated, guilt flashing across her face. "After you told me you thought Gary might've been in your yard that night, I got worried. I parked out front. I just wanted to keep an eye on things in case he came back."

"You were watching my house?" Maggie asked, stunned.

Nicole nodded. "I saw Victor pull into the garage. When he got out, he looked down the street. There was a man in a hooded jacket, just standing there... watching him. I couldn't tell who he was. I wasn't sure if it was Gary or just some random neighbor."

"Why didn't you tell me?"

"I didn't want to freak you out," Nicole said. "But now... after what just happened... I'm almost sure it was the same guy."

The ambulance fell into a tense silence, the only sound the hum of the engine and the distant echo of city noise.

"Let's go—this alley is giving me the creeps. Let's head back to the station. I'm ready to call it a night," Maggie said, brushing her hair back from her face.

"Are you all right? Did he hurt you?" she asked, concern heavy in her voice.

"No," Nicole replied, finally steadying herself. "But I don't think I'll be able to sleep tonight." She took a slow breath, her hands no longer shaking. She shifted the ambulance into gear and drove them out of the alley and back onto the main street.

"Why don't you stay at my place tonight?" Maggie offered. "I'll feel better. Besides, I'm a little spooked now, too—especially after what you said about that guy down the street."

Nicole nodded. "Yeah... okay. That sounds good." The fear from earlier still lingered, and she wasn't in the mood to argue. The idea of being alone tonight was unbearable.

They returned to the station, turned in the keys to the ambulance, and left. Nicole followed in her car as Maggie led the way home.

Maggie pulled into the garage while Nicole parked along the curb out front. As Nicole walked up the driveway, she glanced nervously in both directions, scanning the quiet street for any sign of the hooded man. Maggie closed the garage door behind her, and they entered the house together.

Wrangler greeted them at the door, tail wagging.

"Well, hello, big boy," Nicole smiled, reaching out. She didn't have to bend down—Wrangler's head came up past her waist. He rubbed against her leg, happy for the attention.

"Hey, can you let him out back, please?" Maggie asked, setting down her keys.

"Sure. Come on, let's go outside." Nicole opened the door, and Wrangler dashed into the yard. She shut the door behind him and turned back inside.

Maggie reached for the light switch in the kitchen. "Want some tea?"

"That sounds good, thanks," Nicole replied. She still felt off-kilter, the adrenaline slowly fading.

"Why don't you start the water boiling? I'll grab something for you to wear and set up the couch with a blanket and pillow."

Maggie set a small pot on the stove.

"A T-shirt and shorts will be fine," Nicole said, grateful for the comfort.

Maggie ran up the stairs while Nicole stayed in the kitchen, the water beginning to simmer on the stove. In the bedroom, she pulled open a dresser drawer, grabbed a T-shirt and a pair of loose cotton shorts, then turned to the closet. Reaching up to the top shelf, she tugged down an extra blanket.

As it slid from the shelf, her hand bumped something hard—Victor's locked wooden box. It teetered for a second, then tumbled to the floor with a loud *clack*. The blanket caught in her arms, but the box landed awkwardly, one of the back hinges snapping loose.

Maggie knelt quickly to pick it up. She held it for a moment, debating whether to put it back—but the broken hinge had already revealed just enough to see that the lid could now be pried open without a key.

Her hand trembled as she eased the lid open from the back.

Inside were photographs. Several of them.

Her breath caught.

Her heart sank.

The images were of women, different women—some of them appeared to be unconscious. Some, partially dressed. Her fingers shook as she flipped through them. A ribbon with a butterfly charm lay beneath the last photo.

Maggie stared, frozen. Her stomach churned as her mind reeled, struggling to piece together what she was seeing—what it *meant*. The whisper from earlier—*"Come here, my little butterfly."*

It wasn't just a coincidence.

She clutched the box to her chest, trying to steady herself, her thoughts spinning in disbelief and horror.

CHAPTER TWENTY ONE

Maggie found newspaper clippings tucked beneath the photographs—one about Victor's missing ex-wife, the headline faded but unmistakable. Another, older article featured a grainy image of a young blonde girl—his sister. Maggie's stomach turned as she read the story of her death. Victor had claimed she died in an accident—but this... this suggested something else entirely.

There were more items. Earrings, a silk scarf, a pair of delicate lace panties, and a silver necklace. Maggie's breath caught in her throat. That necklace. Her memory shot back to the Cayman Islands. The young girl on the beach—the one who smiled and said her necklace was "one of a kind." This was it.

She staggered back slightly, her vision spinning. Images came flashing back in erratic succession—the girl at the mall, the taxicab outside the hotel, and the car wreck on the side of the road. Something was wrong. Deeply, horribly wrong.

From downstairs, Nicole heard a thud.

She ascended quickly and stepped into the room, smiling as she spoke, "What'd you drop up here—blankets falling on your head?"

Then she saw Maggie, pale, stunned, sitting on the floor surrounded by the contents of the box.

Nicole's smile faded. "Maggie?" she said more urgently, stepping closer. "What is all this? stuff or—"

Her voice trailed off as she knelt beside her and saw the clippings.

"Maggie?" she repeated, this time alarmed.

Maggie finally looked at her, as though surfacing from deep underwater. "This stuff... it's Victor's." She handed her the newspaper articles with trembling hands.

Nicole scanned the headline about the missing wife. "I thought she *died*," she said, confused.

"So did I," Maggie whispered. "But this... and the necklace. It belonged to a girl we saw in the Caymans. She said it was one of a kind. I—" She stood suddenly, stumbling toward the nightstand and pulling open the drawer. "Mallory. I need to call Detective Mallory."

She grabbed his card and began to dial when the sound of the front door closing echoed up the stairs.

Victor.

He walked into the bedroom, loosening his tie and setting his briefcase down. His eyes fell on the box, its contents exposed on the floor. Then he looked at Maggie.

For a long second, the room froze.

"So," he said calmly, "what are you girls up to?" He shrugged off his suit jacket and draped it over a chair.

Maggie's face was stiff, her expression neutral but strained. "Nicole's staying the night. I was getting her a blanket from the closet. Your box fell. Sorry."

The silence that followed was thick, suffocating.

Victor looked at the open box again. That box was locked."

Nicole stood slowly. Hi, Victor. It s... nice to see you again," she said, her voice tight, eyes flicking back and forth between Maggie and him.

Victor smiled faintly. Is it?"

Victor s eyes lingered on the items as he returned them to the box, his movements methodical, deliberate. Yes, nice seeing you too," he finally muttered, his tone clipped.

Maggie tucked a lock of hair behind her ear, her voice strained. We re making some tea... are you coming downstairs?"

Victor didn t look up. My uncle s here. He s downstairs."

Really?" Maggie said, feigning surprise. You didn t mention he was coming."

I didn t know. He just showed up." He closed the lid on the box, his hand pressing it down a little too firmly. Unannounced."

Maggie nodded slowly, then walked toward the door. Nicole trailed after her, quiet, eyes scanning Victor s expression before she turned away.

They descended the stairs.

In the kitchen, a large man was perched on the counter—denim jeans, sweat-stained tee shirt, and a slouched posture that exuded ownership, not hospitality. His presence filled the room, but it wasn t just his size—it was his smell, his stillness. Something about him felt... off.

Maggie hesitated, then forced a smile. Hi, I m Maggie. This is my friend Nicole." She tried to keep her tone light. It s a pleasure to meet you. Victor doesn t talk much about his family... so, you re his uncle?"

The man grinned, a yellowed flash of teeth beneath a cracked lip. He wiped his hand across his chest, then reached for hers. "Yeah, I'm Bob. Been watchin' my boy for a while. Thought it was time I dropped in."

"Watching?"

Maggie stiffened but nodded, backing toward the cabinets. "Can I get you something? Tea? Coffee?"

He scratched his neck. "A cold beer'd hit the spot."

She opened the fridge, her mind whirring. Nicole hadn't moved from the corner.

Maggie noticed her then—her expression frozen, her posture stiff, and her eyes locked on the man. Maggie followed her gaze and saw it:

A hooded sweatshirt draped over Bob's lap.

Nicole's face had gone white. She didn't speak. Didn't blink.

Bob sniffed loudly and leaned back against the counter. "You girls live here too, or just visitin'?"

Maggie handed him the beer. "Just visiting," she said carefully, voice calm. "Nicole and I work together. Long shift tonight."

He cracked the can open and took a long swig, watching them over the rim.

Victor stepped into the room, loosening his tie. "Everything okay in here?"

Nicole finally spoke, her voice dry, nearly inaudible. "Where's the bathroom?"

Victor pointed down the hallway. She nodded and slipped out of the kitchen. Nicole's mind raced. She tried to call Detective Mallory, but, it went to voicemail.

Nicoles' next instinct was to dial 911. However, Victor recognized her extended absence and knocked on the bathroom door.

It was locked. Nicole, I will break the door; come on, get a move on," Victor said angrily.

Maggie watched Victor follow the hallway after Nicole, then turned back to the man on the counter, who was now watching *her* with unreadable eyes.

Bob, what do you do?" she asked, stalling.

He took another swig. I m in... collections," he said, smiling. All kinds of things people forget they owe."

Victor and Nicole returned to the kitchen, but Maggie s hands were trembling as she set the cup back on the counter.

Tea?"

You know," Nicole said quietly, her voice edged with urgency, I think I should go. That way, you can have a family visit."

She turned toward the hallway, but Victor was already there, blocking the exit. His presence filled the doorway like a wall. Nicole s hope of escape evaporated in an instant.

No," he said, with chilling calm. I insist. You should stay."

His eyes flicked toward Bob, as though waiting for approval, like a dog waiting to be told it had done well. Nicole froze. She stepped back into the room, her instinct pulling her toward Maggie.

Outside, Wrangler barked furiously at the sliding glass door. He jumped and slammed against the windowpane, claws scraping the glass. Bob limped over and yanked the blinds shut with a heavy clatter.

Shut up, dog," he growled, pounding the glass with his palm. "Stupid mutt."

Nicole's breath caught. That voice. That limp. The alley. Her legs threatened to buckle as the recognition hit. She moved closer to Maggie, her arm brushing hers for grounding.

Maggie turned toward Victor. "What's going on?" she asked, voice trembling.

Victor didn't respond. His gaze was far away—glazed and detached—as if he were watching something no one else could see. A butterfly drifted across his memory, landing gently on a pale, unmoving girl's cheek. Emma. Woods. Silence.

"Victor!" Maggie's voice cut through like a knife. "You're scaring me. What is going on?"

He flinched, blinking rapidly as if coming out of a trance. Then his expression hardened.

"You shouldn't have gone digging," he said coldly. "You just couldn't leave it alone."

"That's my boy," Bob chuckled. "She's just like that last whore you married. Can't trust a whore. Come on, my boy—kill the butterfly. Don't let it get away. Like when you were little—remember? Catchin' butterflies in jars." His voice turned guttural. "Come on. Show me what you know."

Victor took a slow step forward.

"Victor, no—no-you won't get away with this," Maggie said, trying to stay calm. "Detective Mallory—"

He cut her off, voice rising like a flame. "Detective Mallory will be busy chasing the lead *you* gave him. About Gary." His mouth twisted into a grin. "Especially when his pretty little sister goes missing."

Bob burst out laughing, a deep, rasping sound that rattled in his throat. He kicked the sliding door again, Wrangler barking violently on the other side.

Victor was advancing.

Nicole and Maggie backed against the stove.

"Please, Victor," Maggie pleaded. "You don't have to do this. You need help. We'll help you. Let us help you."

"Help?" Bob laughed, nearly choking. "You hear that, boy? She wants to help you. Like they helped your mom? Like they helped Emma?" Egging him on.

Victor's face flushed red, his jaw clenched. The air in the kitchen grew thick, every second stretching like wire pulled taut.

Nicole's fingers slowly reached behind her for the kettle on the stove, still hot from boiling water.

As Bob staggered closer to Nicole, she drove her knee up sharply, slamming it into his groin. He doubled over with a grunt. In one motion, she grabbed the kettle of boiling water and hurled it into his face.

Bob screamed—an inhuman sound—clutching his burning skin. Steam rose from his cheeks as he collapsed, moaning in agony.

Nicole darted past him, but Victor was faster. He grabbed her mid-stride and slammed her to the ground. Then he turned—rage ignited—and delivered a crushing blow to Nicole's jaw. She crumpled with a cry, dazed and half-conscious, falling to the ground.

Nicole tried to crawl away, gasping for air, but Victor seized her leg and yanked her back. He drove his boot into her stomach. Her breath vanished.

Maggie, eyes fluttering, forced another kick with her steel-towed EMS boots at Bob s head, making sure he would stay down. Seeing Victor towering over Nicole, she lunged, leaping onto his back. She wrapped her arms around his neck, tugging hard. Victor slammed himself backward against the refrigerator, sending her sprawling. He turned and struck her again—hard—her body slapping the tile floor. Blood trickled from the fragile capillary beds on her brow line.

Bob lay collapsed nearby, his airway scorched, wheezing. His eyes fluttered. He wasn t moving.

Wrangler s barking exploded into madness outside, paws hammering the glass. He instinctively wanted to protect Maggie, his owner.

Victor caught Nicole again. Grabbing her by the hair, he bashed her head into the floor—once, twice, a third time. She went limp. Blood seeped from her nose and mouth.

Panting, Victor released her and stumbled back. For a moment, there was only the sound of his ragged breathing and the dog s muffled howls.

He turned to Maggie.

She was trying to rise, bruised, broken. Victor opened the utensil drawer and pulled out a knife. He walked toward her.

No..." she whispered. Victor, please..."

He raised the knife.

I m your butterfly," she cried. You don t have to kill me. It s me, your butterfly. Emma..."

At the name, Victor paused. His arm trembled.

His gaze clouded, drifting back in time. Sweat and blood blinded his eyesight as he used his shirt to wipe his face. Maggie pleaded louder, it's me, Emma. The woods. The butterfly. His hand wavered in the air.

Then—*thunk.*

His body jerked. His eyes widened. He looked down, breath catching in his throat. The knife protruded from his back.

Victor dropped to his knees, then collapsed forward. He moaned once. And was still.

Behind him stood Nicole. Bloodied. Shaking. Her hand still mimicked holding the handle of she gripped kitchen knife she'd used to end him.

She sobbed. Maggie scrambled to her, wrapping her arms around her as both women collapsed to the floor—broken, but alive.

Moments later, the back door burst open.

Detective Mallory entered, gun raised, radio in hand. He took in the scene in a flash.

"Officer needs assistance! Multiple injuries. I need paramedics now!"

Wrangler's howling finally fell silent.

And in the middle of the blood-soaked kitchen, Maggie and Nicole clung to each other, sobbing, shaking, surviving.

"How did you know to come here?" Maggie asked, her voice cracked with tears as she wiped at her face.

Detective Mallory crouched beside Victor's body, his expression hard but not unkind. "You called my cell and hung up. That was enough." He paused, glancing at her. "We'd already started looking into Victor. We found a partial fingerprint at one of the earlier scenes. He was under surveillance. I was nearby. Just not close enough."

He checked for pulses. Victor was gone—his body lifeless on the tile. Bob was alive, barely, his face blistered and red, wheezing shallow breaths. Mallory radioed for paramedics.

Within minutes, the house swarmed with uniformed officers and EMTs. Nicole and Maggie were both carefully loaded into an ambulance. Bruised, bleeding, and emotionally shattered, they rode side by side in the back.

Nicole lay back with her eyes closed, silent tears leaking down her cheeks. Maggie held her hand, stroking it gently, offering what comfort she could.

As the siren wailed and the city lights passed outside the rear doors, Maggie turned her gaze toward the darkness beyond the window. Her thoughts drifted.

Patricia Castle.

That name—the woman in the alley. The one whose life, like her own, had been shattered in the shadows.

She saw it all again: the sirens, the blood, the night her husband was killed in a dark alley in San Antonio. Another life. Another time.

Now, once again, she was left with pieces to pick up. Trauma stitched into memory. But this time... she wasn't alone.

She looked down at Nicole—still breathing, still alive—and silently vowed not to let this night break her.

CHAPTER TWENTY TWO

Maggie rested her head on her arms, using them as a pillow while lying on the soft park grass. She gazed up into the blue abyss above, watching clouds drift slowly across the sky, their shadows casting moving patterns across the lawn. The ambient symphony of birdsong, distant laughter, and rustling leaves filled her ears. She took in a deep breath, held it for a moment, and exhaled with quiet peace.

A year ago, her life had been unrecognizable—darkened by violence, trauma, and uncertainty. Today, her thoughts and dreams had shifted. There was pain, yes—but there was also healing.

Using her knees, she pushed herself upright just as Nicole and Wrangler came bounding into view.

Out of breath from playing fetch, Nicole collapsed beside her on the grass, laughing as she dropped to her knees. Wrangler flopped down with a huff, panting, tail thumping contentedly.

"Hey, are you doing all right?" Nicole asked, brushing strands of hair from her face as she tried to catch her breath.

Maggie smiled. "Yeah... I'm fine. Everything's going to be all right." She reached over to scratch Wrangler's ear. "He's going to miss you."

Nicole's face softened. "I'm going to miss him, too. But Dallas is just a short drive away, right? Believe me, I'll be back to visit—you'll hardly even notice I'm gone."

"Do you mean it?" Maggie's voice caught slightly, emotion swelling in her chest.

Nicole nodded, her gaze steady. "Really. I swear. I think it'll help Gary, too... being closer to Dallas. He's doing great in the program up there. It's good to see him finally happy. Finally... trying."

Gary had heard about that horrific night the morning after, waking up drunk in an alley, unaware he'd been the primary suspect in a string of violent crimes. Seeing Nicole in a hospital bed, beaten and broken, had jolted him awake—maybe for the first time in years. That same day, he checked himself into a rehab program in Dallas. Now, nearly a year later, he was still clean.

Maggie nodded, eyes glancing past Nicole.

"That's not the *only* reason you're going," she said softly, tilting her chin toward the young woman approaching them.

Nicole turned as Kathy—dark-haired, warm, pale blue-eyed, with a swagger of radiance in the afternoon sun—walked up and offered her hand. Nicole took it, smiling.

"Hey, sweetie. Are you almost ready?" Kathy asked, eyes moving gently to Maggie. "Hi, Maggie."

"Almost," Nicole replied, tugging on her hand and pressing a kiss to her fingers. With a grin, she coaxed Kathy to sit behind her, wrapping her arms around her shoulders. Nicoles' body melted as she released her weight against Kathy's chest.

Nicole caught Maggie watching. For a heartbeat, something unspoken passed between them—an old ache softened by understanding.

Nicole still felt that familiar tug whenever she looked at Maggie, but deep down she knew: this move, this new life—it was right. It was time.

"Don't you two look sweet," Maggie said with a grin, watching them. Her chest ached with the weight of goodbye, but she knew letting go was what love sometimes meant.

Nicole leaned her head back into Kathy's neck. "Yeah, well... if *Kathy* would go to art school, I wouldn't have to move to Dallas."

"Hey!" Kathy squeezed her with a laugh. "You know, there's always room for you *and* Wrangler. And I'm pretty sure you'd have no trouble finding a job in Dallas, Maggie."

Maggie smiled, but her eyes dimmed slightly. "I don't know. Maybe someday."

She stood, brushing grass from her jeans. "You'd better hit the road if you want to beat traffic. Go on—get out of here before you make me cry."

Nicole stood and pulled Maggie into a tight hug. "You know I'll always love you, right?"

Maggie kissed her cheek. "I know, you silly girl. I'll always love you, too."

Made in the USA
Coppell, TX
08 October 2025